LIBERATED

HOLT AGENCY
BOOK FOUR

KALYN COOPER

COPYRIGHT

Liberated

KaLyn Cooper

Cover Artist: Syneca Featherstone

Editors: Trenda London & Erica Scott

ISBN: 978-1-970145-38-0

eBook Published by Black Swan Publishing

Copyright © Published 2023, Black Swan Publishing

Printed in the United States of America

ABOUT THIS BOOK

She was the job and off limits, but his heart wanted so much more.

Heath Kubiak jumped at the chance when a Holt Agency job came up in the Apostle Islands. After years of working back-to-back missions all over the world, he longed to take some much-needed time off. He knew that area of Lake Superior extremely well. He'd take lead of the team this time, they'd find whoever was lost in the National Park, then he'd stay for a week or two, fishing and camping. Sounded like a perfect plan.

All Annali Frantz wanted to do for the summer was get away from teenagers, her parents, and Washington D.C. She loved teaching biology to high school students, but she also needed a break from them. When the opportunity arose for her to work at a research station—and get a full semester credit toward her second master's degree—she couldn't pack her bags fast enough. For the past two years, her mother had been on a mission to find her the right husband for when her father, the senator, made a run for the White House. Ali hated politics, and that's all her dates wanted to discuss. Avoiding first dates and spending time on the Great Lakes with other scientists and forest rangers was the perfect summer plan.

Best laid plans never work out quite right. Will they this time for Heath and Annali?

Dear Reader,

Thank you so much for purchasing Liberated, my second book in the Holt Agency series. Books number one, three, and five are written by Becca Jameson. Heroes and heroines from my books will make appearances in hers, and vice versa. My books are number two, four, and six, the final book in the series blends Holt Agency men and Black Swan Team 2 women.

Speaking of heroes and heroines, you're going to recognize the men of the Holt Agency from Shadow in the Desert and Shadow in the Darkness, both by Becca Jameson, and Shadow in the Mountain and Shadow in the Daylight by KaLyn Cooper. You may wish to read all four of these books to fully understand the complexities of the characters in the Holt Agency series. All of these books are stand-alone romantic suspense and military romance.

Complete links to all of the above books can be found in the back of this book.

I hope you enjoy reading Liberated.

Always,
    KaLyn

For the latest on works in progress and future releases, check out **KaLyn Cooper's website**

Follow **KaLyn Cooper on Facebook** for promotions and giveaways

Sign up for exclusive promotions and special offers only available in **KaLyn's newsletter**

DEDICATION

*I dedicate this book to those who have found the love of
their life in an unusual place or time.*

ACKNOWLEDGMENTS

Thank you, Becca Jameson, my persistent and patient writing partner. This series was conceived almost three years ago. Without Becca's determination this series still might not be published.

I'd like to thank the members of the Black Swan Book Club for their constant support! Special thanks to member Missy Ryan for suggesting Jonah and Meredith for the names for Annali's parents.

I cannot thank my new editors enough: Trenda London for keeping the pace fast and offering ideas; and Erica Scott, for correcting all my Dragonisms, commas, and missing words.

A huge thank you to my publicist, formatter, and right-hand woman, Michelle Duke.

Thank you to my wonderful husband who puts up with deadlines.

CHAPTER 1

"SHANNON, SEE IF YOU CAN GET A HOLD OF SOMEONE AT the National Park Service." Jonah Frantz started barking orders the minute he hit his office door in the Hart Senate building in Washington D.C. "I need them to check on my daughter. She's working at the University of Michigan summer research station at the Apostle Islands National Lakeshore."

"Senator Frantz, has something happened to Annali?" Susan, his press secretary asked, always trying to get ahead of the story.

"Probably not." Jonah grabbed his stack of pink message slips from Shannon, his secretary, and headed into his private office, Susan on his heels. "Meredith is worried sick. Ali missed her weekly call to her mother on Sunday. They have this system worked out that if she misses her mother on Sunday, she's supposed to call back Monday night. It's Wednesday and Meredith still hasn't heard from her."

"I'm sure everything is fine." Susan tapped on her

tablet. "Senator Frantz, are you ready for your morning briefing?" She looked at her watch. "You have ten minutes before you have to leave for the Hill for your committee on energy and natural resources."

Shannon knocked on his door frame, worry emanating off her in waves. "Senator," she called meekly. When he looked up from his desk, she continued, "Sir, the Apostle Islands are not in your jurisdiction. They're actually in Wisconsin."

He let out a slow breath. He didn't give a shit where they were located. He'd been elected by the people of Michigan, but he sat on multiple national committees, including one that dealt specifically with the national park system. He tamped down his urgency for her to do as he'd requested.

He just wanted someone to check on his daughter. "Shannon, Annali is working for the University of Michigan on a research station that just happens to be on one of the Apostle Islands. It wouldn't matter if she were in Texas. I'd still have you contact the National Park Service. Please do that now."

He turned his attention to Susan. "Yes. Go ahead. Start with the most important in case we don't get through them all." As his director of communication started talking, his personal phone buzzed with the text. The caller ID indicated it was a picture from his daughter. He was ready to call out to his secretary and tell her not to bother the National Park Service when he opened the picture.

He stared at the small screen, not understanding what he was seeing. Why was his daughter sleeping on the floor? Were conditions of the research station that bad? Why hadn't she mentioned this before? He'd personally spoken with her last Sunday and she sounded very upbeat, claiming the accommodations were just fine. He knew his little girl was tough and they'd enjoyed camping when she was younger, but she was thirty-three and working on her second master's degree. These accommodations were totally unsatisfactory. He'd personally make the call to the head of national parks.

When she rolled over, he realized it was a video he was watching. The chains fastened to her leg and wrist moved like snakes across her body.

Jonah's heart dropped into his stomach.

No. That couldn't be his daughter.

His beautiful daughter, the high school biology teacher, was chained to a pole in the middle of a dilapidated shack.

"Sir, are you all right?" Susan was standing leaning over his desk. "You went white as these walls."

Before he could answer her, the phone rang. He jumped back as though it were a live venomous snake.

He stared at the phone, not daring to move. If he didn't answer the phone, then it wasn't real. The video of his daughter wasn't real.

It rang a second time.

Susan, who was levelheaded in the worst circumstances, looked at the caller ID and smiled. "Looks like there's your answer." She pointed to the phone where the screen indicated he had an incoming call from Annali.

Jonah shook his head. He must've been mistaken. That must have been something else that was on his screen. She was calling him now.

"Sweetheart, you had your mother worried."

"I don't think we know each other well enough for you to call me sweetheart," the male voice chastised.

3

"Who the fuck is this and where the hell is my daughter?"

At his abrupt words, Susan jumped into action. She snatched the phone from his hand and started punching buttons. It only took a few seconds before she handed it back to him and mouthed *recording*.

Thank goodness someone was thinking straight because he certainly wasn't.

"Senator, such vile language from someone of your esteem. Do you kiss your wife with that mouth? Speaking of Meredith, she's probably having heart failure according to our little Ali here." The man had the audacity to laugh. "You can tell your wife that you've seen your daughter, but I'm not sure I'd share that video with her. From everything I've read, she is rather delicate."

The man was right on both points. No way in hell would he show that video to his wife. She would immediately faint. But God help us all when she woke up. She'd be on the next plane headed to Lake Superior, bound and determined to find their daughter.

"I demand you tell me where you are holding my daughter captive."

The man laughed hard and loud. "Senator, you are in no position to make demands of me. I am going to tell you what you're going to do in just a few minutes. But before we get to that, I have some rules. Rule number one is the most important rule; involve no one. You call the police, you'll never see your daughter again. You call the FBI, you'll never see your daughter again. You involve any kind of law enforcement, and Little Miss Ali will simply disappear. Have I made myself perfectly clear?"

"Yes," Jonah choked out. "What is it that you want me to do?"

"You are the ranking member of the National Parks Subcommittee of the Senate Committee on Energy and Natural Resources. As such, you are going to wholeheartedly support everything that the secretary of the interior is going to suggest today in the budget discussion, especially where it pertains to national parks. It would be even better if you suggested an increase above what they're going to ask for..." The man's tone changed. "Given that you've voted against raises for national park employees every year you have sat on that subcommittee. The other senators followed your lead and stopped even the possibility of raises in the subcommittee. Raises for the hard-working men and women who care for our national parks never even made it to the Senate floor."

Damn it, he was right. But Jonah had dozens of reasons why he voted against raises, starting with the fact that everybody across the board needed to cut back. Not just national parks. There wasn't enough money in the budget to go around. He still believed that he was doing the right thing.

But he'd agree to it, anyway. He would do anything to get his daughter back. "Okay, I'll do that."

"You'd better. I'll be watching you, live. Keep your phone on you. I might decide to send you some more videos or a photograph of your daughter to remind you what you're supposed to be doing." The man chuckled. "You'd better get a move on, Senator Frantz. You don't want to be late."

The line went dead.

Jonah collapsed back into his tall executive chair. "Did you hear all of that?" he asked Susan.

"Every word." She picked up the phone and checked the recording. "We got everything." She continued to fiddle with his phone.

"Wonderful." He felt defeated. "What the hell are we supposed to do with it? He threatened Annali if I went to the police or FBI. What the fuck am I supposed to do?"

Susan handed him back his phone. "You're supposed to show up at that meeting and be there as soon as the cameras turn on."

"Oh, shit." Jonah sprang from his chair and searched his desk for the meeting folder.

She handed it to him. "I sent the recording to my phone." She signaled him to move. "We'll walk and talk." Surprisingly, she kept pace with his long stride. "I may have an answer. You know that my boyfriend is on the vice president's staff." She looked around as they turned a corner. Whispering, she continued, "His son got into some trouble in Africa a few years back and as a result the vice president has a close working relationship with a group of former SEALs in Indiana. If you'd like, I can call my boyfriend—"

"Yes. Call him right now. Have him text me the information. I'll be in this meeting for at least an hour, and probably two." Jonah quickly said goodbye to his press secretary and increased his stride to make it to the room in time.

Thirty minutes into the meeting, his phone rang. Damn. His staff knew not to call him. He hoped it wasn't the kidnapper because he'd been trying like hell to show his support. He wondered if the man had any idea of the formal protocol adhered to even in committees. He checked the caller ID and was shocked to see Office of the Vice President.

"Excuse me, Mr. Chairman, but this is an emergency call…from the White House." Without waiting for the formal dismissal, Jonah stepped out into the hall. "Senator Jonah Frantz speaking." He was relatively sure that it was Susan's boyfriend on the other end, but just in case it was someone else, he decided to be formal.

"Jonah, I hear you're having a bit of difficulty." Oh. My. God. It was the vice president.

"Yes, sir. Did someone explain my situation to you?" He glanced around the hallway, happy to see no one was nearby in case he had to tell them everything.

"Yes, and I saw the fucking video. I have just the men to find your daughter and punish that fucker."

CHAPTER 2

HEATH KUBIAK TOOK THE CHAIR BESIDE KENNER LANE AT the large mahogany conference table at the Holt Agency office in southern Indiana. At the far end, Larson Aldrich sat behind multiple computer screens, glancing up only to nod in acknowledgment as each man walked in.

"Morning, Pitbull. Viper. Keebler." Keene Soto, better known to them as Gramps, strode in with a smile on his face.

"Obviously married life is treating you well." Kenner slapped him on the shoulder as he passed by. "How are Kelly and Jock doing?"

Heath didn't know it was possible, but Keene's smile grew even wider. "They're both great. Jock hit a homerun last Saturday. It was his first." He had puffed up as proud as any father.

"Does anybody know why we got the 911 call?" Heath asked.

Without looking up from his computers, Keebler announced, "Trek and Birdman are on the phone with

Washington now. The vice president called Ryker about seven-thirty this morning, then they talked to a senator. When they called all of you guys in, they assigned me to research the Apostle Islands." Larson pointed at the large flatscreen on the wall behind the head of the table as a map of the Great Lakes appeared.

Heath smiled as he stood. "The Apostle Islands are right here." With his index finger he circled the area west of the Upper Peninsula of Michigan and north of the small amount of shoreline Wisconsin has on Lake Superior. "Wisconsin, for as big a state as it is, only has about a hundred and fifty miles of shoreline on Lake Superior. Michigan, on the other hand, is totally surrounded by the Great Lakes, touching all but Lake Ontario. It has the most waterfront on Lake Superior thanks to the U.P."

He pointed to Bayfield, Wisconsin, on a piece of land jutting into Lake Superior. "My grandfather has a fishing cabin near here." Heath couldn't hold in the smile. "I spent a lot of my summers up at the fishing cabin with him."

"What the hell do they want us to do all the way up there?" Kenner asked.

"Rescue the senator from Michigan's daughter," Ryker announced as he walked into the room. "Show them the video."

Heath settled back in his chair to watch the video. All the men sat in complete silence as they viewed a woman chained to a pipe in the middle of a rustic cabin. As she rolled over, they could see her bloodied wrist and ankle. Her long brown hair covered most of her face, but Larson held a freeze-frame that showed just a glimpse of what lay beneath. Her cheek was reddened as were her eyes but those looked to be swollen from crying, not abuse. But that didn't mean her captor, or captors, wouldn't start beating on her, especially if her father didn't do as instructed. It was always harder for the victim to recover if they been severely beaten.

They'd been sent on so many of these rescue operations over the past three years. Not that Heath would ever become numb to a woman's suffering, but this one hadn't gotten nearly as bad as some they'd seen. They'd also been called in early in this situation. Hopefully, that will help them find her quickly and return her to her parents.

Ryker announced, "We have a recorded conversation between one of the kidnappers and Senator Frantz." They then listened, and re-listened, to the phone call several times, each man making notes then comparing. Often one man would pick up a slight intonation that might help them narrow down the kidnapper's identity.

Heath had to admit, this was the first time a kidnapper had ever required the parent to actually do something positive. In every other case he'd been involved with, the kidnapper's end goal was money. "This man didn't ask for money, so it makes me wonder if he hadn't thought it completely through. Could it have been a snatch and grab based on convenience?"

"Possibly." Ryker nodded. "That would support the theory that he knew Annali."

"Larson, run the video once again, please," Kenner suggested. As it played, he asked, "Heath, are all the shacks like that?"

"Relatively. The cabin could be anywhere in that area. There are some homes, nice ones, that have been well kept since 1970 when the National Park Service established the islands as a national lakeshore. People still rent those houses." Heath shook his head. "There are twenty-one islands spread out over about seven hundred and twenty-five miles."

"Did you just say twenty-one islands?" Keene asked. "I might be a backsliding Baptist, but last I know there were only twelve apostles in the Bible."

Heath shrugged. "I have no idea."

"I can confirm there are twenty-one islands covering only seven hundred and twenty square miles," Larson corrected. "You need to update your data, Heath. I've been looking at this information for nearly fifteen minutes and I can't tell you why they were named the Apostle Islands."

"For our purposes, it doesn't matter." Ryker demanded every man's attention. He nodded to Larson who posted the daughter's driver's license and official school photograph.

Heath sat up to take a good look at both pictures. Seldom did anyone's driver's license make them look pretty but hers did. Her annual school picture, on the other hand, made her look gorgeous. Both showed off her big brown eyes, the color of well-aged whiskey. Intelligence shone through even in her government picture.

"Annali Frantz is a high school science teacher, biology primarily, in one of the D.C. suburbs," Ryker continued with details. "She is working at the University of Michigan research station, which is based on Stockton Island. But she travels to all the islands taking water samples, checking game cameras, collecting bugs, and probably more things that her father didn't know about. He was quite distraught, as you can imagine."

"I don't know if there still is, but when I was a kid, there was a ranger station on Stockton Island, at least during the summer. Several other islands have docks maintained by the National Park Service. Mostly, they service the lighthouses and campgrounds," Heath continued. "There was also a small airport on Madeline Island, and a few rental properties, mostly on the inner ring islands. Those are easier to get to, and back to the mainland should bad weather kick up."

Larson picked up with more details. "People canoe and kayak out to several of the closer islands for picnicking and primitive camping, but the National Park Service doesn't recommend the use of canoes, open cockpit or sit-upon kayaks, or paddle boards for travel between the islands or in the sea caves. Lake Superior's powerful waves and unpredictability of storms make that type of small craft too dangerous. There's a ferry service that makes regular runs to some of the islands and a tourist ferry that leaves Bayfield twice a day taking visitors to Devils Island, which has some of the more popular caves. Water taxi services are also available."

"Can we rent boats?" Xena asked as she strode into the room and took her seat beside her husband, Ryker. "I'm going on this one. My Navy experience will be helpful and given our target's possible mental condition, she might need a friendly female face." It wouldn't be the first time Xena had been on a Holt team. She had the same SEAL training as the Holt agents and more in certain areas. She was always an asset and never let the fact that she was married to Ryker get in the way. Xena was a complete team member.

"What do we know about the kidnapper?" Keene leaned forward with his elbows on the table.

"Nothing, for sure." Ryker opened the bottle of water

in front of him and took a long pull. "We speculate that he's a national park ranger given his demands."

"That doesn't bode well for us," Heath pointed out. "If he's been stationed there for a while, he'll know those islands well. There are lots of places to hide. Many of them are riddled with sea caves. There's even a small lake on Bear Island you can dive down into and come out in Lake Superior. There's lots of forests on the islands to hide in, as well as dozens of old fishing camps."

"Do we have a contact at the National Park Service? Is someone getting us a list of all the park rangers assigned to Apostle Islands national lakeshore?" Keene suggested.

"Senator Frantz is supposed to be getting us that information," Ryker said. "Hopefully Larson will have it, and complete bios, on each by the time we land."

"Do we have access to thermal satellites?" Kenner asked.

"We've been promised some satellite images by the time we land," Ryker continued to explain, "but I've been warned that it's summertime and there are a lot of unregistered people who camp on the islands. Especially locals. They just hop in their boats and drive out to the islands, pitch a tent, and enjoy camping."

"No one answered my question." Xena cocked her head and stared at her husband. "Can we rent power boats? That way we can divide up and cover more territory."

"Larson, look into that for us. I was going to suggest using jet skis, but I think we'd be better off with bigger boats," Ryker ordered.

Heath laughed. "We're talking just a few miles from Canada. The water temperature this time of year barely gets up to fifty degrees. I don't want my ass on a jet ski in freezing water. I wasn't kidding when I said waves on the lake can quickly reach four to six feet."

"I think we're going to need a bigger boat." Kenner deepened his voice, humming the *Jaws* movie music.

"On it. Big boats. Big motors." Larson clicked on the keys then answered without looking up. "I'll have water transportation for you by the time you arrive." This time the company's computer guru looked up. "Weather is supposed to be good for the first twenty-four to thirty-six hours then turn to shit. Island extraction could be dangerous. Be sure to take enough inclement weather gear and food to sustain you at least a week without resupply."

"Fasting, my favorite thing to do," Xena commented facetiously as she patted her hips. "I could stand to lose a few pounds."

"You're beautiful just the way you are." Ryker leaned over and gave his wife a sweet kiss.

Xena patted his cheeks. "You have to say that. You like sex."

"I think every person at this table likes sex," Heath noted. "Some of us just don't get it as often as others."

"Poor baby, Pitbull." Viper threw his arm around his friend. "Do we need to make a trip to the bars in Louisville, Kentucky as soon as we get back?"

At the mention of returning to Indiana, Heath spoke up. "Ryker, after this mission is over, would you mind if I took a week of vacation? I'd like to go to my grandfather's fishing cabin. Maybe do some hiking, fishing, reading. Basically recharge."

"Fine with me." Ryker tilted his head as though thinking. "You haven't taken any vacation since we started the company almost three years ago. I'd say you're long overdue."

"Thanks." Heath immediately started making a mental list of other things he'd need to take besides their standard search and rescue gear.

"Viper, how soon can you have the plane ready?" Ryker asked.

"I need to get my personal gear together then prep the plane," Kenner replied. "Unless there's something else we need to discuss here, let's plan on being wheels up in an hour and a half."

"We're done." Ryker stood. "If anymore intel comes in between now and then, we'll brief on the plane."

Heath walked out beside Kenner. "If you need help prepping the plane, I should be able to assist you in thirty minutes." Heath was close to qualifying to fly the company's jet. The overly generous gift from Zesaro Neberu had arrived shortly after the Holt Agency had completed another successful mission for the owner of several gold mines in Ethiopia. "Thanks, I'd appreciate that." Kenner nodded. "How close are you to getting certified?"

"If we'd stay home long enough so I could get more flight hours with the instructor, I'd be done in a few weeks." Heath had been fast tracking his flight education. He'd learned to fly props while in high school and had his private pilot's license before he graduated. In the Navy, only officers flew airplanes and as an enlisted SEAL he didn't have that opportunity. He was working hard to be instrument qualified as well as jet qualified. After this mission, he would go to Indianapolis and spend a solid week or two finishing his instruction.

Until then, fortunately Kenner had gone to Navy flight

school before getting an eye injury during a pickup football game. He'd really enjoyed SERE school, the military's survival, evasion, resistance, and escape training, so he decided to become a SEAL officer. Even though he no longer qualified to be a Navy pilot, Kenner went ahead and finished his civilian jet license. The man could also fly helicopters.

As they took off for a small Air Force reserve base in Duluth, Minnesota, everyone settled in for a pre-mission nap. As Heath tucked the soft pillow under his head and covered himself with the warm blanket that matched the interior of the plane, he thought briefly of Annali on the cold hard floor, thin blanket, with no pillow in the brief video. And the chains.

Hang in there, Annali. We're coming for you.

CHAPTER 3

ANNALI FRANTZ ROLLED OVER ONTO HER BACK TO GET OUT of the rays of the mid-morning sun pouring through the east-facing window…only to be stopped short by the chain attached to her left hand and left foot. The restraints were only long enough for her to reach the camp toilet in the corner and the cooler of food always left several feet inside the door.

Damn. I must've been drugged again.

Whatever they were using was damn potent. She'd been out for nearly twenty hours. Again. She hated the residual dry mouth and brain fog. But it could have been worse. Much worse. She hadn't been raped or beaten. She wasn't sure why, but the side of her face was sore for the first day or so. It wasn't feeling bad today.

She sat up slowly and leaned against the pole while she got her bearings. She was tethered too tightly to reach any wall. As she glanced around the twelve- by fifteen-foot rustic cabin, nothing had changed as far as she could tell.

Ali listened to the family of red squirrels scampering

over the thin roof before she managed to stand. Once she was sure of her balance, she shuffled her way to the camp toilet in the corner. Before she used it the first time, she'd scanned every nook and cranny looking for video cameras. Unable to find any, she'd since felt much more comfortable using the leave-no-trace facilities.

As far she could tell, she was on day four, provided she hadn't slept a full twenty-four hours under the drugs the first day. As usual, a midsized hard plastic cooler sat just within reach, a few feet inside the door. The blue and white one from yesterday was gone. She wasn't sure when or who brought her food and water every day, but it magically appeared by the time she awoke each morning.

She was normally a light sleeper, awake at every noise and shift of her condo, but since her capture she'd been out cold and long every night and much of the day. After the second day, she figured something in the cooler was being drugged because within an hour after her one and only daily meal, she would fall sound asleep and be out until the next morning. Yesterday, she left the ham and cheese sandwich, thinking that probably contained the sleeping medicine.

She was wrong.

Today, she'd eat the sandwich and the fresh fruit, but would thoroughly inspect the water bottles. She hoped it wasn't in those. She needed the water to stay hydrated.

She would also wait until she was absolutely starving before she ate anything. She needed her brain to clear. She needed to think. She couldn't even remember how she got to the cabin. Hopefully, by putting off eating, her head would be clear enough to remember how she ended up in the cabin chained to a metal pole that seemed to hold up the roof. She remembered similar poles in the unfinished basement of her parents' house in Marquette when she was very little.

The memory of roller skating around the outside of the poles and weaving through them from one side to the other made Ali smile. Well, at least her early elementary school memories were accessible to her. Perhaps others would soon be also.

She was a little hungry and needed to put something in her stomach. Near as she could figure, she hadn't eaten in twenty hours. She shuffled over to the cooler and sat down on the half-century-old wooden floor. There were two different kinds of sandwiches today, one bologna and cheese on white bread and the other deli turkey on whole wheat. Thankfully, there were several condiment packets of ketchup, mustard, and mayonnaise. She hated dry sandwiches.

There was an apple, a banana, and an orange. Nice. Three pieces of fruit today. Ali loved fruit.

Wow. There was even a premade salad and a packet of dressing. She wondered if her captors lived on the mainland and shopped for her every day at one of the delis.

As she stared at the oversized plastic lunch cooler filled with more food than they'd ever brought before, she worried that perhaps they weren't coming tomorrow. Or ever. Maybe they'd decided she was too much work. To be on the safe side, she'd only eat part of the food and drink half the water. Just in case.

She carefully inspected the crisp green apple, looking for an injection site. Not seeing any, she delicately bit into it and examined the piece before she ate it. Her brain was clear enough to get started and she was over being scared.

She decided to start with the premise that somebody had kidnapped her and needed to keep her alive.

Who would be missing me by now?

That was easy. Her mother. If her mother had been home on Sunday night, and she usually was, Ali would have certainly missed their weekly phone call. Her mother had insisted she get a satellite phone and call every Sunday night at nine p.m. Eastern time. If, by some weird chance, they missed each other on Sunday, she was to call again on Monday at nine. If she missed again, then Tuesday, then Wednesday, etc. If Ali was correct, today was Wednesday and her mother would be going ape shit crazy. They'd never missed their Sunday night call in the three weeks she'd been in the Apostle Islands. Her mother probably had her father calling out the National Guard. She was relatively sure that as a senator he didn't have the power to do that, but a little detail like that would never have stopped Meredith Frantz.

Who else would be missing her?

Hopefully the other researchers would have noticed that she hadn't returned in days, but maybe not. Several students were only there for two weeks and some for thirty days. There were even a few who were at the research station for six weeks. Only a few of them working on a master's program were there for all eight weeks of the summer. Howard and Cliff had been there since early May and would be there through late September. Several had already rotated out.

She remembered watching a few of the undergrads pack and thinking she had another few days before they left. She was walking out the door to go check the outer islands.

20

It was just a snippet. Like a mental picture. Was that a recent memory? Or was it weeks old? She'd seen several students come and go.

Damn. She wished she could remember.

Focus. Who else would realize she was gone?

She wondered if Dr. Kaczynski even read the reports that she wrote so diligently every single week. If he did, perhaps he'd realize she was gone when she didn't send in her reports on Saturday. Or had she sent in her reports on Saturday? She distinctly remembered exchanging the mail pouch with the mailman.

Damn. Damn. Damn. Was that this past Saturday or was she remembering a previous exchange? She'd done it several times, that she remembered. Nobody else wanted to carry the large satchel down to the dock and bring the new bag to mail. Yet everyone was hopeful they'd receive care packages from home.

Ali enjoyed the simple task, though. Several of her students had written to her. Every couple of weeks she'd catch a ride back to Bayfield on the mail boat. She'd treat herself to a meal in town, pick up personal supplies, and spend the night in one of the quaint little B&Bs or a hotel. The ability to soak in the bathtub and wash her hair in hot water was a luxury she afforded herself on her days off. It also gave her the ability to upload several of the pictures to her Instagram account. She was shocked at how many former students had been following her that summer.

Thinking about washing her hair made her head itch. Since she was chained, and bottled water was precious to her, she hadn't been able to wash much of anything. On day three, she'd sacrificed one of the water bottles and a napkin in her daily lunchbox. By the time she had finished wiping off the important body parts, the napkin was in shreds, but Ali felt a hundred times better. The Lake Superior islands were nowhere near as oppressively hot and muggy as D.C., but they'd been experiencing an exceptionally warm start to summer.

Returning to her quandary while her mind was still functioning, her next question to ponder was who kidnapped her and why? She was just a high school biology teacher. Most likely, it was because of her father.

But we're not rich. My parents don't have millions of dollars. For years it seemed as though all their money went into their father's campaigns. First, while he was a representative from the Upper Peninsula to the state legislature. After they'd moved to Grand Rapids, he'd run for the House of Representatives and won. Several times. But again, it always seemed as though their money went toward his next campaign, which was every two years. While she was in high school, he switched to the Senate and won his seat. Campaigning now only happened once every six years. Her parents did seem to have a little more money, but they certainly weren't millionaires.

Was there any chance that her captors thought the money her father had in his campaign chest was his? If so, that person was a fool. They obviously had no idea how expensive a political campaign was—even one to get reelected. Technically, that money wasn't his. He couldn't use it to pay her ransom.

It was a good thing no one had asked her for money. She just barely made enough to pay for her tiny condo, make payments on her four-year-old car, and eat. Ali was thrilled when she found out that this was a paid research position in addition to giving her an entire semester's worth of credits, enough to finish her second master's degree.

Ali stood and gazed out the two windows. The cabin was back in the woods. That's probably why it had lasted as long as it had. If it sat on the beach, it would have been destroyed in the first huge storm. Smart fishermen built their cabins a couple hundred feet into the woods. Logically, they were close to a safe harbor for the fishing boats. That only left a dozen or more islands as possibilities. She could hardly see anything through the woods, not even a path.

The woods were so dense, she couldn't feel the wind to help her determine which side of the island she was on. Not that wind direction was always a good indicator. The Apostle Islands were located in such a unique position that the wind could not only come from the west, but it was not unusual for storms to kick up out of the east or swoop down from the northeast out of mainland Canada.

As she took the last bite of the apple, she sat down and leaned against the pole once again. She wondered who was taking care of her experiments, if anyone. It had been her job to travel to each island in the ancient powerboat to take water samples at the same places every day. Then she would run the boat onto a beach and tie it off while she went to each game camera and pulled out SD drives. It was her job to copy the drive onto her tablet, making note of everything from weather conditions to time of collection.

After replacing the drive into the camera, she then scanned the area for wild animal scat. That was literally a shitty job, especially because if he found any, she had to collect it in plastic bags and label it properly. Sometimes she had no idea what kind it was but after a week on the job, she could unequivocally confirm that bears do shit in the woods. Often. Especially if they had been eating berries. Runny purple bear poop was not fun.

She could also guarantee that bears stink worse than a high school boy's locker room. Her second week on the island, Howard and Cliff asked her if she wanted to go bear hunting with them. They were both working on PhDs dealing with bears in the Apostle Islands. There had been a report that a bear had been seen on Cat Island. Not unusual because most of the islands had bears from time to time.

She'd been part of the deer project in West Virginia one summer, so the men had invited her along. Cat Island was only about two and a half miles long and three quarters of a mile at its widest point. They were able to find the bear and Howard shot it with a tranquilizer dart. Between the three of them, they were able to quickly take all the measurements and attach a tag to the animal, so they'd be able to track her movements. They quickly left the island, wanting to be long gone before the bear woke up.

Ali once again examined her chains. They looked to be the only thing new in the whole bare cabin. Even the portable camp toilet was showing its age. Luckily for her, the seat was still in one piece and all three legs were in working condition. Hers was the type that had a plastic bag hanging underneath a bent hanger to hold toilet paper. After the second day, someone took the plastic bag daily. She was so thankful they had because it had started to attract bugs.

The hardest part, she'd decided, was the boredom. Even though she was only awake a few hours a day, it was more than enough to have examined every inch of the cabin. Ali was used to talking constantly all day long. She taught six classes each day and during her lunch, she talked with other teachers.

If her calculations were correct, she hadn't spoken to another human being in four days. She missed talking with people.

CHAPTER 4

"All secure." Heath helped Kenner with the final check of the company plane while Keene unloaded all their gear, staging it to be loaded as soon as Ryker and Xena arrived with their rental vehicle.

Heath gathered the equipment he wouldn't need until after the mission and set it aside. "This can go in first and stay in the SUV because I won't need it until we've rescued the senator's daughter."

"Are you keeping the vehicle?" Keene asked.

"Yes. I'll take you back to the plane before I go to my grandfather's cabin."

The married couple pulled up in an extra-large SUV. Loading was accomplished within minutes with everyone helping Heath with his extra gear then loading their own.

"GPS says we should be there in just under two hours," Xena announced from the driver's seat, so Ryker could brief everyone while on the road.

"We just got this satellite map." Ryker turned his computer around so all three men in the back seat could see. "These were taken around four this morning. The analysts believe these are the most likely possibilities. No one is registered for primitive camping on those islands, but like Heath told us before, not everyone fills out the paperwork."

"Some of these families have been going to the same islands for a hundred years and others don't even own a computer," Heath added.

"They're scattered on almost every island," Kenner pointed out.

"We knew this was going to happen. That's why we've booked two motorboats," Xena said as she pulled out onto a major highway heading into downtown Duluth.

"Heath and Kenner, you're team bravo. Xena and I are team alpha." Ryker's gaze met Keene's. "Gramps, you're going to run the local ops base. Larson has booked rooms for us all at a bed and breakfast right next to the pier. I hope you all got some sleep on the way up here because we're going to be hunting all night. The plan is to check out all these possibilities first and as fast as we can. Larson said there's a storm moving in tonight."

"It's not safe to move between the islands at night without a local guide and we can't take that chance. The islands aren't lit up and only a few of them have light-houses. It's too dangerous." Heath pointed to the furthest island to the east. There was only one place circled. "Outer Island is the most remote and the least used by tourists. Most of them stay to the inner ring islands. The kidnapper isn't going to try to keep her someplace where she might be discovered accidentally."

"Makes sense," Kenner agreed.

"In case anybody is interested, we are now leaving

27

Minnesota and entering Wisconsin to save the Michigan senator's daughter," Xena announced as they crossed the bridge. "I hope that gives everyone their geography lesson for this afternoon."

"Thanks, sweetheart." Ryker leaned across the center console and gave her a quick kiss.

"Stockton Island is one of the more popular and that's where her research camp is located." Heath pointed to several islands. "Depending on where he kidnapped her, Outer Island is relatively convenient. And it's one of the biggest."

"Fuck. Looks like we're going to be tromping through the woods at night," Kenner grumped.

"We brought night vision goggles, and yes, they're the ones with thermal," Keene reminded everyone. "Hourly check-ins on the sat phones."

"Yes, Dad," Kenner teased.

"I suggest we don't kit up until we reach the island. Way too many tongues will wag if we step onto motor-boats with weapons strapped to our thighs carrying long guns." Heath glanced at everyone's clothing. "Let's wear what we have on."

"We'll go to Manitou Island. That one has two possi-bilities," Ryker announced. "It's a pretty small island so if we don't find her at either of these two places, there might be enough daylight left to check out Otter Island."

"Sounds like we have a plan." Keene nodded his head at each team member.

Two hours later, they were checked into their B&B, meeting in Ryker and Xena's bedroom to sort through the gear.

"Larson gave us a heads up that the front is moving

through faster than expected. It should be here just before dark so be sure your raingear is handy." Ryker had several piles sorted out on their bed. "Everything stays in the waterproof bags until we reach the islands. Even though the picture doesn't show anyone with her, somebody had to be holding the camera and we don't know how many are standing behind him. Expect a hostile situation."

"Yes, sir," replied both Heath and Kenner.

"If you find her before we do, be prepared with plenty of water and food." Xena put several pieces of camping gear into one of the big duffel bags. "Little sips. Small bites. We don't know what she's had to eat or drink since she was kidnapped most likely four full days ago."

Kenner yawned so hard his jaw popped. "Do you think we should go interview the people at the research station? Maybe we can get a better feel for where she might be kept."

"That's a damn good idea." Ryker slapped him on the shoulder. "And you are the perfect person to do that." Kenner got his nickname, Viper, during an interrogation. Someone had found a venomous snake and he'd used it to encourage answers from the Taliban while they were on a mission in Afghanistan. "You're tired after flying all the way here while we napped. We'll get another boat for you to take to Stockton Island. Heath, you're on your own for this first one. Tomorrow, you'll team up with Kenner as we check the next several islands. If there's more than one hostile, wait for backup."

"Yes, sir." Heath had been on solo missions before. All of them had been. He was only checking out one possible hut. The image inside it was so small it could be animals. He just hoped it wasn't a bear that decided to make an old fishing cabin its new den. Except for bears and white-tailed deer, there weren't any large mammals on any of the islands.

By the time the four of them made it to the docks, a third motorboat had been ordered. Since the rental agreement said they would be keeping the boats for several days, they were required to take a thirty-minute safety briefing. Kenner asked about navigational equipment and before they left, they'd all downloaded a more detailed island map.

Heath hated to lose that half-hour of daylight, but they had to make their cover look plausible.

"I'll lead since I've been here before," Heath announced. Careful of what they said in front of the locals, the four team members waved goodbye and hopped into the three boats. Once they passed Basswood and Madeline Islands, about ten miles from Bayfield, they pulled together.

"At the next island on your left, Hermit Island, you two are turning left and then veering right," Heath instructed, and they all followed on their maps. "I'm heading straight from here. I have at least another ten miles before I reach Outer Island then another two to where I can secure the boat and start my inland hike. I promise I'll call in every hour." So they wouldn't all try to call at the same time, they'd preset team times. Heath was still team bravo, so he was to call at the bottom of the hour. Kenner was team charley for tonight and he had quarter after, while team alpha had the forty-five minute mark. If anyone missed their calling time, they were to phone at the top of the hour.

"Good hunting," Ryker called as they shoved the boats apart.

Heath pushed the power lever all the way down and trimmed up the boat, so it skimmed across the relatively smooth surface. By the time he reached the tip of Outer Island, the waves from the east were getting choppy and nearly three feet high. There was nothing to break the wind for nearly a hundred miles of deep cold lake. He could see dark angry clouds building over the deepest part of Lake Superior off toward the shores of the Michigan Upper Peninsula.

He took the west side of the island to use it as a barrier against the increasing wind and fast approaching storm. The southern tip was a spit of sand extending two thousand feet as though it wanted to reach out and touch Stockton Island four miles away. The western side had sand and rock beaches that led nearly to the lighthouse on the far northern end. Luckily for Heath, he didn't have to go quite that far. He could run the boat onto the shore and tie it to one of the large trees that kissed the shoreline. His goal was a clearing a hundred and fifty feet up a small creek before dark.

He'd only made it halfway down the island and when the little remaining daylight had been completely covered by dark gray clouds. Heath slipped into his head-to-feet raingear, tying his hood just as the first drops fell from the sky. Within minutes it was pouring in sheets. He could hardly see his navigational gauges. Purposely, he was skimming close to the edge because he didn't want to miss the small creek. When he saw the island abruptly curve to the right, and white water splashing from the hillside into the lake, relief washed through him.

By the time Heath secured the boat, Lake Superior was kicking up waves over four feet tall. The mouth of the stream certainly wasn't a small craft safe harbor, but it was the best he could do. He carried his waterproof bags several feet into the dense woods. It would keep everything dryer than in the open boat. And it was safer, just in case the boat decided to go for a ride without him. It also kept additional weapons and ammunition close.

As he geared up, selecting which weapons to strap to the outside and which ones to hide inside under his layers, he scouted the ground. He was more concerned about human footprints than those of bears. Unfortunately, it had been raining long enough that even in the deep woods footprints would have been washed away.

Just to be careful, Heath found a fallen pine tree and hid his extra bags. He needed to travel light, not knowing in what condition he'd find Annali Frantz, if she was there. What had initially looked to be a hundred and fifty feet turned out to be closer to two hundred fifty feet. Thank goodness for night vision goggles. The rain had swollen the creek, making it impossible to walk up. It also soaked the surrounding woods, challenging him to slip and slide on every step. What should've taken him less than ten minutes had taken nearly an hour in the relentless rain.

The cabin in question should be right around the bend.

Heath's watch alarm vibrated.

Damn. It was his time to call in again. He certainly didn't want to walk back to the lakeshore to try to get a satellite and lose all the distance he'd gained, so he pulled out the larger phone and parked himself close to the trunk of a pine tree. Extending the antenna, he dialed base.

He was shocked, and thrilled, when Gramps answered the phone. "Thank Christ."

"Team bravo, checking in, quack quack. Nothing is moving around in this downpour, except me. Even ducks are tucked in for the night."

"Please tell me you're off the lake." Keene sounded worried.

"Affirmative. I'm approximately two hundred feet inland next to a gushing creek. Fifty feet from probable target." Heath knew if the high-value target wasn't in there, he was going to curl up and make it his home for the night. "Everybody else secure?"

"Yeah. Viper checked in here about forty-five minutes ago. He's asleep in the next room. He promised a full report tomorrow when he catches up to the three of you but said nobody knew anything. Ryker and Xena decided to bunk in the second cabin they checked." Keene chuckled. "They found a squatter inside the first one. From what they said, the man had moved in. He had a beach lounge chair, a solar-powered cooler, and even a fancy biodegrading toilet behind a hanging sheet."

Both men laughed at the image.

"I'll call you back if I find the HVT. If the cabin is clear, I'll bunk down there for the night, but I'll call him one last time. Team bravo, out."

CHAPTER 5

ALI SAT CROSS-LEGGED ON THE FLOOR IN ONE OF THE FEW dry spots in the cabin where her chains would allow her to reach. She was a little bit hungry but didn't dare eat anything that was left in the cooler. Something in there contained the drugs that knocked her out for twenty hours at a time. She was determined to stay awake. She was done being imprisoned in this rundown leaky shack.

Night had fallen quickly but that was most likely due to the storm, which must be a fierce one.

She'd been in the islands long enough to have seen several storms. They weren't that different from the ones of her childhood on the Michigan Upper Peninsula. She and her grandfather would stand on their dock and watch the correlation between clouds, rain, and waves as he answered every one of her questions. Even as a child she'd had a curious mind. She was sure she'd gotten it from her grandfather. She'd followed him into teaching science, but she'd chosen high school rather than at the university level. Maybe someday, she would also be Dr. Frantz.

She hadn't thought about her grandfather in months. It must be the storm. She smiled at his memories. She missed him.

Shivering under the thin blanket, she wished she was standing on the dock in front of their research station watching the curtain of rain move across the lake. Even when they lived in Grand Rapids, they had a house on Lake Michigan. The storms were nowhere near as ferocious as on the U.P., but that never dulled Ali's fascination of the uncontrollable power of nature.

She and her father had long talks about global warming. She could argue both sides while her father was a firm believer that the earth had existed for billions of years and weather temperatures were cyclical. He thought the New Zealanders were absolutely ridiculous for wanting to tax farmers for the burps and farts of cattle.

Maybe Congress should fund a study on the comparison of burps and farts of cattle with those of dinosaurs. Can you imagine how bad dinosaur farts smelled? I'm quite sure a herd of Supersaurus put more methane into the atmosphere every day than a herd of cattle. That was her father's favorite argument, and in truth, he might not be wrong.

A huge drop of water fell on her forehead and dripped off her nose. She ran her hands on the floor all around her looking for a dryer spot before moving. She suspected the Coast Guard had issued a small craft warning. Normally, she would have been warned hours before the storm hit, giving her plenty of time to return to the research base. She always carried a small battery-powered radio with her tuned to the emergency channel.

I wonder where's my backpack? And my boat?

35

She sucked on the tip of her index finger in an attempt to dislodge the sliver she'd gotten while loosening the floorboard. Ali smiled in the absolute darkness. One of the best parts about not eating the drugged food was that her mind had started to clear and the desire to escape had increased.

Once she determined that there was no way in hell she was ever going to dislodge the pole, nor was she going to find the weakest link in the chain and pull it apart and escape, her next best option was to fight back. Her kidnappers wouldn't expect to find her awake when they returned the next morning, or if they showed up during the night. Unless she was going to beat them over the head with the camp toilet, which she discovered was bolted to the floor, she needed to find a weapon.

She'd paced every inch of the cabin that her chains would allow. When the board rocked under her foot, she had her weapon. It took hours to loosen it by standing on it and rocking. Using her short-clipped nails, she finally tipped up one end and dug the board away from the others. She'd been giddy when she discovered a nail had come with it.

She had a weapon.

Now, if she could just stay awake until her captors returned, she would fight back.

As the storm raged, Ali wondered if they could get to her. Were they camping somewhere on the island? Was she on one of the many islands or had they taken her to shore? There were hundreds of miles of barren shoreline in both directions with only a scattering of small towns between the Apostle Islands and Minnesota. East to Michigan was the same way. Hell, for all she knew, they could've taken her the two hundred miles to Canada.

Damn! Why can't I remember my kidnapping? Where was I when they took me? How far did they take me? How many captors are there? Why take me now?

Ali had too many questions and not enough answers. Until she could capture one of her kidnappers, she had no way of finding out. What did she really need to know? Thinking the situation through logically, if she were able to surprise her captor and knock him out, what would she do next?

The sound of rain pelting the door changed. It lessened but the rest of the cabin was still being pounded.

Someone, or something, was in front of the door.

Ali jumped up.

Where should I stand?

Damn. She hadn't measured the distance of her reach with the board in relation to the door. She quickly positioned herself as close to the door as her chains would allow.

She wished she could see the door handle, but the storm didn't have any lightning. Only rain-filled clouds determined to empty into Lake Superior. She'd never been awake when they entered so she didn't even know if the door squeaked.

She felt the gust of wind that carried pelting rain with it.

She raised the board above her head, nail pointed outward, intent to pound on anything that touched her.

"Annali Frantz?" The deep male voice called her name. She hadn't heard a single spoken word in four days.

"I'm here to rescue you, ma'am."

Ali stood frozen. Should she believe him? Was he one of the men who had kidnapped her? How many men did it take to capture her? She couldn't remember, damn it.

"Ma'am, please put down the board." His request was followed by a gust of wind that soaked the front of her clothes.

How the hell could he see her board? She couldn't see him so how could he see her?

"Ma'am, even if you're not Annali Frantz, I'll get you out of here. Please, though, I need you to put down that board so I can come in and close the door."

She lowered her arm.

"Ma'am, please throw the board off to your left."

If he actually was there to rescue her, she was wasting time, so she tossed the board. It hit the wall and fell to the floor.

"Thank you, ma'am. I'm going to come in now." He stepped in, closed the door, and backed up against it, out of her reach. "Are you Annali Frantz?"

She nodded her head and then realized he couldn't see her. The cabin was pitch black. "Yes." The word came out as a squeak. She tried again, but she hadn't used her voice in days. "Yes. I'm Ali." At least this time it was distinguishable enough to her.

"Ms. Frantz, I'm Heath Kubiak. Your father sent my team to rescue you."

Her knees gave out and she crumpled to the floor. She couldn't stop the tears from starting. "Are you really here to take me home?"

"Yes, ma'am." The words came from right beside her. "Are you hurt? Hungry? Thirsty?" It sounded as though he was digging in his pack when suddenly a light came on.

He had a flashlight. Illumination brightened her soul. She didn't realize until that moment how terrifying it was to sit in the dark.

Now she could see him opening the pockets of his backpack.

He handed her a bottle of water then took out a second one and set it to the side. He closed that pocket and opened the one right under it. This time, he handed her a protein bar.

She tore into the plastic using the residual light and bit off a huge chunk. Chocolate. Oatmeal. Granola. Heaven. And best of all, she doubted it was drugged.

Starting at her feet, he ran the flashlight slowly over her body. "Are you hurt anywhere, Ms. Frantz?"

She shook her head because her mouth was full of goodness. She swallowed then confessed, "My ankle and my wrist." She stared at the cuffs attached to the chains. "You don't happen to have a handcuff key, do you?"

His grin slashed white in the shadow. "Yes, ma'am. I do." This time he stood and took off his rain poncho. Reaching into his back pocket, he pulled out a small key. "Your hand, please. After I get these off you, I have some salve I'll put on the wounds then I'll wrap them."

He set his flashlight in a bendable device so it shone on her wrist, freeing his hands. Holding her hand gently as he twirled the tiny key round and round, his fingertips lightly brushed her palm. "As soon as I get you out of these handcuffs and dress your wounds, I need to call into base and let them know that I found you." Still twisting the key, he smiled at her. "Is there any message that you'd like us to send to your parents? Besides the fact we found you?"

Ali hadn't thought anywhere near that far ahead. Of

course, she'd like to tell her parents...what? That she couldn't wait to get home? The thought of leaving her summer job, abandoning her research, never finishing her degree, horrified her. The more she thought about it, she didn't want to leave. She was rescued. Hopefully they would find whoever kidnapped her and once the threat was eliminated, there would be no reason for her to go back to Washington. She could stay, finish her work, and get her next master's degree.

"You have a little bit of time to think about it," the man said as he freed her wrist from the chain.

She'd never felt such relief wash through her body as she did when she could pick up her left hand without the weight of the chain. "Thank you." Her voice was hoarse and raspy.

She wanted to reach out with both hands and pull him into a hug. But he'd already leaned away toward her ankle and repositioned the light.

So many questions ran through her mind at the same time, but she settled on what she considered to be the most important. "How do we get out of here?"

"My boat is tied up at the end of the stream about two hundred and fifty feet from here." He looked over his shoulder at her. "I'm really sorry but we're not going anywhere until the storm passes."

"Where am I?" Ali was happy that her voice was getting stronger with every sip of water.

He stopped twisting the key and light blue eyes the color of a sunny day reflected on the lake looked back at her. "You're on Outer Island, the northwest side."

Ali let out a deep sigh. Then she giggled. "That's good.

I was afraid that maybe they had taken me to Canada, and nobody would ever find me."

The chains clinked as they fell off her ankle. She immediately raised her leg and wiggled her foot in all directions. She could feel the smile on her face and joy like she'd never felt before deep inside.

Her rescuer was back in his pack. He untied the large green roll with a red cross in a white circle on the front. She'd never seen anything like it before. It had everything from surgical equipment to butterfly strips. He seemed to know exactly what he needed.

"What have you had to eat?" he asked as he extracted a tube of something, gauze pads, the extra bottle of water, and surgical tape.

"Every morning there would be a cooler of food waiting for me over there." She pointed closer to the door. She felt the need to explain, "Something in the food is drugged. Within an hour after eating, I fall asleep and don't wake up until the next morning. I never hear them coming in, and I'm usually a much lighter sleeper."

He poured water over a gauze pad and gently took her hand in his, lightly cleaning her wrist. "Have you ever seen your kidnappers?" He touched the sensitive skin over her wrist bones, and she automatically tried to jerk her hand away. "I'm sorry, but I need to clean your wrist as well as possible. Do you know that alcohol or hydrogen peroxide would delay your healing?" He continued to tenderly wash the abrasions.

She felt like an idiot. "I had no idea. I figured alcohol would probably clean it better." Then she remembered his earlier question. "No. I've never seen them." She thought about the plural use. "I don't know if it's just one person or several." Feeling helpless, she dropped her free hand into her lap. "I'm sorry. I'm not much help. I can't even remember where I was when I was kidnapped. What I was doing. Nothing. I wonder if the drug they used on me made me forget."

The man squirted something clear onto his finger and gently smoothed it over the reddened areas of her left wrist. "That's very possible." He wrapped gauze around her wrist then ran white tape over it to hold it in place and help keep it dry. "Did they hurt you?"

"Do you mean did they rape me? No," she said with determination because she would have known had they violated her. "Beat me? Not that I know." She touched her cheek where it had been painful the first day and a half. "Maybe. If they hit me, it was when I was unconscious. This is the only thing that has hurt, other than my wrist and ankle."

"After I bandage your ankle, I'll take a better look at that."

"I wonder what happened to my boots?"

"It's a common tactic with kidnappers. If you don't have shoes in backcountry, you can't move nearly as fast so even if you escape, you won't get far." His explanation seemed unemotional, as though what kidnappers did was a common subject for him.

Maybe it was. That was probably why her father had sent them. "Mi—" She was tired of thinking of him as *the man*. "Sir, I'm terribly sorry, but I've already forgotten your name. I think you told me when you were standing out in the rain. You did tell me, didn't you?"

From the area around her ankle, once again, he flashed her those beautiful blue eyes. "I did, but I totally understand that you've forgotten it. Your brain was concentrating on self-defense. My name is Heath Kubiak. Your dad hired us, the Holt Agency, to find you."

"How long have you been looking for me?" She wasn't sure she wanted to know the answer.

"We got the assignment about nine-thirty central time." He wrapped her ankle then sat back on his heels.

"How did you find me?"

He stared at the half-eaten protein bar and water bottle in her hands. "I'll answer that question in just a minute. What kind of food have you been eating?"

"Well, Heath, to be honest, they've actually been feeding me well, except for whatever drug it is they laced my food with that knocks me out within an hour. There's fruit and deli sandwiches, and always a couple bottles of water."

He nodded and smiled. "You're very lucky you had thoughtful kidnappers." He nodded toward the bottle and protein bar. "Go ahead and finish those. If you hadn't been eating at all, or very little, I wouldn't let you eat anymore."

She looked at her hands as though she'd never seen them before. She couldn't believe the food he'd given her just a few minutes ago was already half gone.

He pulled out a satellite phone considerably larger than her own. "Have you thought about what message you want to give to your parents?"

She managed to smile. "Yes. Tell them thank you for sending you."

CHAPTER 6

"T<small>EAM BRAVO CHECKING IN,</small> I <small>HAVE THE PACKAGE.</small> I repeat, I have the package." Heath smiled at the petite schoolteacher who looked to be about his same age. "Healthy except for a few abrasions on her left ankle and left wrist where she'd been handcuffed to chains that were wrapped around a metal pole attached to the wooden floor and leaking ceiling. Treated the abraded joints."

"Good work, Pitbull." He could hear Gramps's smile in his congratulations. "What's the message to be passed on to the senator?" No attempt would be made for contact between Ali and her parents until she was safe on shore or perhaps even headed home.

Ali leaned toward the satellite phone and spoke loudly. "Tell my dad I said thank you for sending your team." She hesitated a second before she continued, "Tell them both that I'm fine and that I love them." She slid back to her original position.

"Ms. Frantz told me that sometime before daybreak the

kidnappers would appear and bring her a cooler of food." He looked at her for confirmation and she nodded.

"They must take the other one away because it's gone and there's a new one in its place each morning," Ali yelled from a few feet away.

"Gramps, did you get all that?"

"Yes."

"Even though it's raining like hell, I don't want her to be here in the morning. Do you see any other huts or anyplace we could go?" He looked at her bare feet, dug out the pair of strap-on sport sandals and socks they carried on rescue missions, and handed them to her.

"There's the lighthouse about a mile north but I have no idea if you can get inside it." Keene was quiet, only mumbling, for the next several minutes. "It looks like there's another shack, about the same size as the one you're in, fifteen hundred feet south down the lake and up another stream about fifty feet. Given the trouble you had getting there, are you sure you want to try to get to this other hut?"

"I know I don't want her here at sunrise." Heath held her gaze. She had intelligent brown eyes and a girl-next-door face. None of his science teachers ever looked that pretty.

"I can make it. I sure as hell don't want to be here when they arrive in the morning." Ali had shocked him with her language. He figured a high school teacher, who was also the daughter of a senator, would be prim and proper, never swearing.

"That'll give me a chance to check on the boat. It should be flatter walking down near the shore. Any chance this storm is letting up?" The storms on the lake he

45

remembered from his childhood seemed to come in waves separated by lighter rain.

"Can you make it to the mouth of the creek in this downpour in forty-five minutes?" Keene sounded doubtful. "If so, it's supposed to let up for about an hour. Still raining, but not this hard. Be sure you're inside before the next one starts. It has steady winds at thirty miles per hour and gusts up to fifty miles an hour."

Heath looked to Ali. "It's about three hundred and fifty feet of slippery, steep creek bank. You'll be hanging on to trees and limbs and anything else you can grab."

"I'd rather be anywhere else but here." She stood to make her point.

"We're leaving now," Heath announced. "Bravo team out." Once again, he dug in his bag and pulled out a Frogg Togg suit for her. The lightweight, breathable material was one hundred percent waterproof. He'd guessed her to be a size small, but he had a medium in his bag just in case.

He attached a barely visible, motion-activated camera in the corner that faced the door. It would feed video directly to their satellite phones and to the Holt Agency computers back in Indiana.

Over the past three years, they'd done so many kidnap and human trafficking rescues that they had refined their list of necessities to carry. Since they had information about her ahead of time, they'd estimated her to be a size small. Unfortunately, they didn't have anything waterproof for her feet.

Barefoot, Ali went to the cooler provided by her kidnappers and grabbed the two gallon-sized plastic bags, tossing out the ice cubes. She returned to the dry spot on the floor and using the blanket, wiped off her feet before she slid on the socks. She put the plastic bags over her socks then strapped on the shoes, making sure the Velcro held tight.

Genius. Heath made a mental note to add plastic bags to their growing list of rescue mission necessities.

She slid on the thin waterproof pants. They were a bit long until she tightened the Velcro on the bottom hem. It helped seal the plastic bags covering her feet. She winced as she tried to slide her left hand down the jacket sleeve, so Heath helped her.

"Your left shoulder is going to be sore from where you tugged on the chains. When we get to the other cabin, I'll give you a topical lotion to rub into it." Heath knew how painful her body would be from being restrained. He'd spent three months as a POW of rebels in Ethiopia.

"Thank you." She eagerly zipped the jacket and secured the hood.

He could tell she was anxious, so he grabbed his backpack, slid the waterproof rain cover over it, and hiked it to his shoulders. "Hang onto my belt. Grab what I grab. Step where I step."

"Got it." When she latched onto his belt, the surprising warmth of her fingers as they wrapped inside his pants at the small of his back sent an unexpected shiver through him. He'd personally rescued dozens of women and given them the same instructions, but no other woman had the same effect on him as Ali.

"Let's go." As soon as he opened the door, the wind shoved at them both. He leaned forward and stepped onto slick, rain-soaked grass. He had to make it fifteen feet through horizontal rain that felt like tiny needles jabbing at his exposed cheeks before they reached the

47

woods where they had saplings to hang onto. They slid with each step but soon learned to walk in sync, steadying each other. When they reached the woods, he was able to use the trees to help balance and move much faster. His goal was to reach the lake by the time the rain eased. The best path back was close to the rushing water, which was now waist deep, looking more like rapids than a creek.

He and Ali were working exceptionally well together, making very good time when her left leg slipped during a large step.

She let go of him, grabbing at the surrounding small trees. Most were too large for her to hold onto.

She slid into the gushing creek.

"Fuck!"

Heath jumped forward, grabbed a strong sapling, and held out his free hand. Flailing in the whitewater, their wet hands brushed but neither could get a good grip.

"I'll meet you downstream," she yelled as she maneuvered her body, feet first, arms crossed over her chest, hands fisted under her arms, chin on her chest.

She knew exactly what to do and had the wherewithal and strength to move into the correct position.

I wonder if she whitewater kayaks? Or enjoys river rafting? Very few people know what to do if caught in a fast-moving river.

It took Heath, moving as fast as he could now that he was alone, almost twenty minutes to reach the lake. Ali sat on the southern bank just inside the woods.

"Are you okay?" he called from the other side of the creek.

She grinned ear to ear. "That was one hell of a ride.

I'm wet, but not too cold. It is easier to get to this side closer to the lake."

"Stay there. I have more bags to retrieve," he yelled above the crashing lake waves. It wasn't until then that he looked up the shore and saw nothing but waves.

His boat was gone.

The ragged ends of the ropes he used to tie it to two trees rode the white froth of waves a few feet offshore. Waves taller than a room rushed toward the shore, curling over onto themselves before they flattened out on the thin strip of sand. The water was immediately sucked back into the lake with the same power that created the next huge curl.

As a SEAL, Heath had spent a lot of time on, in, and under the oceans all over the world. The Great Lakes could whip up the water to rival any ocean storm with waves over twenty-five feet tall. More than three hundred and fifty sunken ships, some buried under thirteen hundred feet of water, were a testament to the rage of Lake Superior during a storm.

"Looks like it's letting up." Ali stood as Heath approached, huge duffel bags over both shoulders. "There's a game trail that runs along the shore about ten feet into the woods."

"Thanks for scouting that out, but you really shouldn't have moved once you reached safety. Had you fallen into the lake, I wouldn't have been here to rescue you," he chastised.

"Yeah, that would've sucked. That undertow is a killer." She smiled up at him, her face glittering with small raindrops that fell vertically. "I can't thank you enough for the waterproof flashlight. It came in real handy when I got close to the lake." She glanced toward the woods. "And when I explored while waiting for you."

"You're welcome." Heath glanced over her. "Were you hurt? That water was really moving."

"No. I'm fine." She grinned. "I believe the depth of the water kept me above the rocky bottom. I floated on top and kept to the center. I knew if I got close to the shore, it would scrape me across those trees."

She led him to the animal trail, and he took the lead. She slid her hand around his belt this time. He missed the warmth of her fingers through his shirt and T-shirt.

"Do you whitewater kayak or raft?" he had to ask as he started down the well-worn trail.

"Both." She gave him that grin again when he looked over his shoulder to check on her. "I did a summer internship a few years ago in the Great Smoky Mountains. One of the guys on our research team paid for his undergrad by guiding on the Pigeon River during the summers. The first time he took me down the river on a raft, I fell in love with whitewater. He taught me how to kayak and that summer we did the Ocoee, Hiawassee, and the Nantahala—that's a cold river I'll never do again. I joined a water rafting club at school, and we did the Snake River in Wyoming, Gauley River in West Virginia, and the Rogue River in Oregon before I graduated. As a graduation gift, Dad and I did a rafting trip on the Colorado River." She turned the tables on him. "Do you whitewater?"

Heath chuckled. "If it's water, I do it. You don't happen to scuba dive, do you?"

"I love to dive. Even my mom dives. We used to take two weeks at Christmas and go someplace with sunshine up. My grandfather loved the Caribbean." There was warmth in her voice as she spoke.

"Did he teach you how to dive?" Heath knew their conversation kept her mind off the misery of the rain and her lack of real shoes.

She giggled and he thought it was the most wonderful sound in the world. "No. Dad insisted we all learn at the local YMCA from a certified master diver."

"Smart man." Over the years, he had met more than his share of people who claimed to be instructors and were extremely dangerous underwater. He was very careful now who he went down with.

"Every dive was a science lesson. Grandpa Frantz taught earth science at the University of Michigan so every time we went down, I either got a lesson in fish, coral, or geography" Ali sighed.

"Do I need to slow down?" Heath was afraid he was walking too fast, so he turned to look at her.

"Heavens, no." She gave him a small smile. "I just miss my grandpa. He and I did a lot of things together when I was young."

Heath turned and continued walking. He kept an eye on the time. Provided the cabin was where Keene said it would be, it might only be another fifteen minutes. "What kind of things do you and your grandpa do together?"

"Everything. We used to, anyway. He passed away in my senior year of college. But we used to have the best time. When we lived on the Upper Peninsula, he and my grandmother had a small cottage on Lake Superior. Grandpa had a sailboat and he and I used to take it out on the lake. He also had a fishing boat and he taught me to fish…after I dissected my first worm."

"I take it you weren't one of those queasy little girls." Heath was so proud of how she was keeping up. They were going to make it to the other shed a few minutes before he'd planned, given that it was exactly where Keene had said it would be.

"No way in hell." She giggled and it touched his heart.

What a woman. Here they were, tromping on an island during a huge storm, basically running from kidnappers, and she could find something joyous.

"I couldn't wait to get back home and dissect the fish we caught," she continued her story. "That's what Grandpa called it. Dad informed me I was cleaning the fish so we could eat it for supper." She giggled again.

He liked a woman who could laugh at herself.

Heath could see a much smaller creek ahead and turned upstream. They hadn't gone far before he found the small clearing and the fishing hut.

"Stay here, hidden in the woods," Heath ordered.

Ali gazed up at him as though he were crazy.

"It's the middle of the night and we don't know if anybody is in there. This might be where your kidnappers are staying."

She visibly shivered.

He put his hands on her shoulders. "You'll be fine, right here. You're far enough back into the woods no one can see you as long as you leave your flashlight off."

"No shit, Sherlock." She cocked her head to the side. "I see you're armed." She looked at the pistol strapped to his thigh.

"Always." It was the truth. The minute he got dressed in the morning until he crawled in bed at night.

"Do you have more than one gun?" She looked hopeful.

"Yes. Can you shoot?" Heath wasn't sure he wanted to leave her with a gun.

"Yes. My personal carry is a Smith & Wesson Shield, the forty-caliber version." She went on to explain, "Often I'm out here taking samples, most often by myself, so I open carry on my thigh." She swallowed hard. "The kidnappers must've taken it from me. But I don't remember. I don't remember anything about my kidnapping or the kidnappers."

The worry in her face made him pull her into his arms. "Getting kidnapped isn't your fault. Don't start blaming yourself. I'm sure you were drugged. Unfortunately, one of the favorite drugs of kidnappers is Rohypnol because it gives the person partial amnesia from the time it's ingested." He hated to ask, but this was a good segue. "Are you sure you weren't raped?"

She nodded against his chest then tilted her head back to look into his eyes. "Yes. That was my greatest fear when I first woke up. All my clothes were still on, but I felt down there anyway. I wanted to make sure. I can't guarantee they didn't touch me, but I didn't have any pain or find any sign of sexual contact."

Without thinking, he squeezed her tighter. "I'm glad for that."

She giggled. "Me too. Now, back to that gun. Are you carrying an extra?"

Heath reached inside his rain slicker and grabbed the Smith & Wesson he'd put into that holster. "It's a forty-five caliber so it's going to kick harder than yours. Hold onto it so you don't drop it the first time you shoot. *If* you have to shoot. And for fuck's sake, don't shoot me." He checked the chamber before he handed it to her, butt first.

He was impressed when she slid the action back and checked the chamber then ejected the magazine to count the bullets. She slid the gun into her coat pocket. "No need to get it wet."

"Stay behind this big tree until I come back to get you." One of the wonderful things about the Apostle Islands was that no one had cut the trees in over a hundred years. They weren't nearly as large as elsewhere for their age because of their short growing season, but a hundred-year-old tree was large enough to hide Ali.

Heath flipped his NVGs to thermal and slowly scanned the entire area. Small animals huddled together to conserve their heat and stay dry. Nothing as large as a human could be seen. He still approached the cabin with caution. There was a padlock on the outside of the door. The small but powerful set of bolt cutters that he carried made quick work of the lock. He cautiously opened the door, scanning the area. Not even a mouse. He flipped up his goggles and turned on the flashlight.

"Perfect."

CHAPTER 7

WHEN ALI STEPPED INTO THE CABIN, THE FIRST THING SHE noticed was that the floor was dry. Hallelujah.

She shined her flashlight around the one-room hut, and then it was suddenly flooded with light. Heath sat on his heels in the middle of the room with a battery-operated lantern that filled the room with glorious light. After spending so much time in the blackness of the other cabin and the darkness of the woods illuminated only by their small flashlights, the bright light emitted by the small lantern warmed her body.

She noticed that the boards were nowhere near as worn as where she'd been held.

"Take off your coat. We'll hang all our wet stuff here." Heath stood next to the door and flashed his light over a wall to highlight the mounted coat rack that looked like something made in a high school wood shop. The pegs angled into the board seemed sturdy enough. She followed his lead and slipped off the wet bottoms, letting everything drip onto the dry wood floor.

A chill ran through her. Ali suddenly realized how wet her clothes were underneath.

As though he read her mind, he suggested, "if you'd like to get out of those clothes, I have T-shirts and sweats I think will fit you."

"You thought of everything." She didn't want to strip in front of a complete stranger even though he'd just most likely saved her life.

"Not just me. All the men and women in our company." He handed her sweatshirt and sweatpants, a T-shirt, clean socks, and a microfiber towel. "I'm going to turn around and put up a clothesline for our wet things. I doubt they'll dry out in this humidity but it's worth a try. When you've changed, let me know."

He turned his back to her and continued to dig in one of his bags. "Rescuing women is one of the things the Holt Agency does. We learned after the first time we rescued women who had been captured for human trafficking to carry clothes and easy slip-on shoes." He shook his head as though in disgust. "Some of the women we've rescued were kept naked."

Ali's heart broke not just for the women they'd liberated, but for Heath and his team. She could imagine men like him discovering naked women. He seemed so... gentlemanly. Professional. Always concerned about her health and well-being.

While she slipped into the heavenly dry T-shirt and sweats, she got a good look at him. The man was built. His blonde hair was most likely from a Scandinavian heritage. As comfortable as he seemed around Lake Superior, she wondered if he'd grown up in Minnesota. Scandinavians were one of the first to settle that area. His navy blue

Henley shirt stretched tight across broad shoulders and around large biceps that rippled with every movement.

Yum. Ali's libido had a soft spot for well-developed biceps. Very few men in the sciences hit the gym or were into outdoor activities. That was probably why she didn't date much in college. Most of the boys in her classes didn't physically appeal to her. She had a short-lived affair with one of the guys in the whitewater raft club until she discovered that he didn't believe in monogamy. Neither did most of the other members in the club. As they camped out next to whatever river they were tackling that weekend, most would pair up, not necessarily with the same person each night.

Ali, her grandfather, and her father had done a lot of camping together, so she wasn't concerned about pitching her tent away from others…and their sex noises. Tents had thin walls.

Completely dressed, Ali continued to stare at Heath. "Were you in the military?"

"Yes. I was a Navy SEAL."

"That explains a lot." Not just his skills in rescuing her, but his body. "How long ago did you get out?"

"Almost four years ago now." He'd affixed a sturdy rope across one corner of the cabin. He hesitated before he asked, "Are you finished changing clothes?"

She felt embarrassed because she'd been standing there gawking at his impressive back and awesome backside. "Oh, yes. I'm sorry. You can turn around now. And thank you for the clean dry clothes. Once I get back to the research center, I can wash them and return them to you so you can use them for the next person you rescue."

He smiled and shook his head. "No need. Those are

now yours. I'm quite sure the cost of the clothes is included in the fee your father is paying the Holt Agency. I think Serena orders them by the dozen. Why don't you bring those wet things over and hang them up."

Ali felt like a fool. A fine male specimen like him was most probably married. "Does your wife work at the agency with you?"

He gave her a knowing grin as though aware she was fishing for personal information. "Serena, who runs our back office, is married to Ajax, one of the company founders. The other founder, Ryker, is here on this mission with his wife, Xena. She's a kick-ass agent. Once we get you back to the mainland, you'll meet her and the other members of this team."

Ali took a minute to look around before she asked her next question. "Nice. We have beds. Kind of. At least I won't have to sleep on the floor tonight."

Heath pulled out a bag the size of a large cantaloupe. "I have sleeping bags for both of us." He tossed the red one to her as he opened the blue one. Shaking it out, it immediately grew and filled. "I have a couple solar blankets in here. I'm going to sleep on top of my bag and cover with one of these." He stood and handed her what her grandfather called a space blanket. She opened the sandwich-sized bag and started unfolding the durable Mylar blanket that was large enough to fit a twin-sized bed.

"We used to carry a couple of these in our car when we lived in Michigan, especially up in the U.P. You had to be prepared for everything in bad weather." Ali had chosen the bed along the north facing wall and laid out her sleeping bag.

"Unless you feel like using the water from that stream, which is carrying a lot of dirt from the top of the island, I have these so you can clean up." He handed her a packet of wet wipes.

Ali laughed. "Baby butt wipes?"

"Don't knock it." His grin was irresistibly self-deprecating. "Right after Serena had the baby, Ajax had some of these with him on a mission in Costa Rica. The mother and teenage daughters we'd rescued were extremely appreciative of them, claiming they were on par with the makeup-removing towelettes. We all agreed they were much nicer to our skin than the ones we'd been buying. It's been baby butt wipes ever since."

She opened the pack and inhaled the smell of infants. "Do you have children?" Given his age, he could have easily been married, fathered children, and was single once again. She wondered if he'd ever answer her previous question about his marital status.

"No." He took something out of his pack that crinkled. "My jobs haven't been really conducive to a relationship. When I was in the Navy, we'd sometimes get called out with less than a few hours' notice. Girlfriends don't like that. Add to it that we were never allowed to tell them where we were going, how long we would be gone, or even give them an idea of when we'd be back. There was a lot of secrecy involved. When we got home, it was the same situation. We couldn't tell them where we'd been or what we'd been doing. It's not a lot different working for the Holt Agency."

He shrugged. "One part is different; I don't have to take the job. There are half a dozen men who work for the company. Not all of us are required on every job." He held up a handful of bags. "Pasta beef Bolognese, ramen with chicken, chili, gumbo, chicken salad, or if you're a vegetarian I have multi-bean salad or pasta with vegetables in butter sauce."

"Do you mean I get to have hot food?" The thought of it made Ali's mouth salivate. "I've been living off cold deli sandwiches and fruit. I'm a carnivore, not a vegetarian. I eat salad and vegetables because I know they're good for my body. May I please have the gumbo? We used freeze-dried food packs similar to that, but not quite as high-tech as those seem, on multi-day rafting trips. Mostly, we cooked over a campfire." She sighed. "That's one of the things I like about this research center. We can have campfires."

"Sorry, that's not going to be possible tonight." He sorted through the packs, picked out hers, and grabbed one for himself. "These will take about ten minutes." He put the foil packets into larger ones and activated the heater with a little water. "While these are cooking, I'm going outside to put up cameras like the ones I left back at the other cabin."

"You left...like a game camera there?" She hadn't seen him put one up.

He walked over to her with his hand out. "These are temporary cameras. They only last a couple days and feed directly to our satellite phones and to the computers back in Indiana."

The cameras were about the size of three half dollar coins stacked on top of each other. "Do they run constantly or are they motion activated?" Ali picked one up and examined all sides. She pointed to the tiny, coiled wire.

"These are motion activated, set for anything human size. Otherwise, we'd be chasing butterflies. That tiny piece of wire is the antenna that will transmit to the satellite." He looked out the foot-tall windows running along two sides near the ceiling.

The cabin was built for this part of the country. The roof overhang protected the windows, yet they would allow a great deal of light into the cabin during the day.

"I hate that you're going back out there in the rain, but thank you for setting up the cameras." She liked knowing that they would be alerted if the kidnappers came to the cabin, or a bear.

True to his word, Heath was back in less than ten minutes.

"You mentioned Indiana, is that where you're from?" she asked as he took off his rain gear and hung it back on the pegs.

"That's where I live now." He checked his watch. "Let's give the food a few more minutes." He dug in one of the other duffel bags and pulled out two more bottles of water, handing her one. He lifted the table from the wall and dropped the leg before scanning his flashlight around the room. When he shined his light into the rafters, he smiled. "Whoever built this cabin intended to use it and be comfortable." He handed Ali a folding lawn chair that would have been too high for her to have reached before he grabbed the other one for himself. "Shall we eat at the table?"

"I want to hug whoever found this place. An actual chair to sit on. A real table. Yes. I want to sit in a chair, at a table, and eat hot food." She positioned her chair at the table and put her water bottle on her side. While he was opening the hot bags, she took his bottle and set it on the other side in front of his chair.

"I hate to be on the phone when I eat but I have to call into base and run a check on the cameras I just installed." Heath set a steaming bowl of gumbo in front of her. He stepped back to his bags and brought her several packs of crackers before he extracted his food and brought it to the table.

"This smells magnificent. I can't thank you enough. It was wonderful just being rescued but you've thought of so many other things." She was so filled with gratitude that she stood and hugged him, fighting tears.

Damn. She hadn't cried except for the first time she woke up all alone and chained to that fucking pole.

Heath wrapped his arms around her and pulled her tightly to him.

It felt wonderful to be held by a man. This man. She caught a whiff of food and dropped her arms. The hot meal was more important than the hot man.

They both sat down at the same time. Ali was almost drooling as the steam of her gumbo rose toward her face. She inhaled a deep breath of deliciousness before taking the first bite. She didn't even try to hold in the moan of pleasure as warm Cajun flavors exploded in her mouth. She chewed a piece of real meat so slowly as to savor every second.

They ate a few bites before Heath pulled out the satellite phone. "Team bravo checking in. We made it to the second cabin and checked into the Ritz-Carlton compared to the Motel 6 where she had been held. Cameras are set up at the old cabin as well as the new one and we are eating a hot meal on a built-in table. This place even has lawn chairs."

Ali silently agreed with him as she took another bite of gumbo with just enough spice to be interesting.

CHAPTER 8

HEATH WATCHED ALI SAVOR EVERY BITE OF HER GUMBO AS he talked to Gramps. They first ran tests on the cameras he'd left at the kidnap hut, as he'd come to think of it. He continued to eat his chicken and rice while talking with local base operations.

Watching her eat so primly in such a rugged environment seemed incongruous. He respected her tenacity. She'd been kidnapped and drugged but was in the process of trying to save herself when he arrived to rescue her. He then dragged her through a stormy night, let her slip into a roaring creek, and couldn't save her so she saved herself, yet she seemed to take it all in stride.

He knew something she didn't; she was going to crash when it all caught up with her. Heath hoped he was the one there to hold her and comfort her. She was an amazing woman, one he'd like to get to know better on a more personal level. Under different circumstances.

As he'd watched his teammates find incredible women, it had made him think about the future. Ajax and

Serena already had one child and he'd heard rumors they were trying for another. Ryker found his equal in Xena, and Tavis and Colette were now living happily in Washington D.C. Keene had moved Kelly and her son Jock into his house on the property he'd bought from Frank and Nancy Holt, on the same Indiana farm as the Holt Agency headquarters. Holden had married Melanie from their Panama Canal cruise and they, too, were living in D.C.

Heath was one of only three bachelors left from the original platoon of eight SEALs. All three remaining single men had been among the six captured by Ethiopian rebels and tortured as prisoners of war for three months before Ajax and Ryker, and Xena, rescued them.

Watching the love his friends had for their women as they settled down to a normal life made Heath wonder if there was a woman out there for him. He hoped so.

With all the cameras working, sending data to Keene back at the hotel in Bayfield as well as to Larson in Indiana, Heath was ready to say good night.

"We're finishing our meal now. How much longer is the storm supposed to last?"

Keene let out a long slow breath. "That's the bad news. It's stalled over us. I walked down to the Coast Guard station and talked to the senior chief there. He thinks they'll have a small craft warning out for at least twenty-four more hours. He said depending on how soon the lake settles down, will determine when they'll lift the warning. You're not the only one stuck. He showed me a list of all those camping on the various islands. There's easily a hundred people out there. There are three families camping on the sand at the south end of Outer Island. Xena and

Ryker made their last check-in hours ago after making sure their boat was still secure."

"Did you tell the Coast Guard that my boat was missing?" Heath wondered if they'd find it adrift or if it had broken into pieces.

"Of course. I'm not a dumb fuck, you know." Keene sounded tired. Heath didn't know what time Viper would wake up from his nap and relieve him but was glad he was back at base to help out. "Speaking of boats, at least we have Viper's boat safely in the harbor. Once we get the all-clear, we can use it to come and collect all of you if we must. The senior chief said they're required to check on every registered camper, including those staying at the B&Bs and house rentals. You're not even on their radar since we never checked in with the national park rangers."

"Good; we don't want to be on anybody's radar until Ali is safely back on the mainland and hopefully, we've caught her kidnappers." Heath didn't tell Keene anything he didn't already know.

"While I'm on the subject of boats," Keene said, "the Coast Guard found one of the research boats floating empty between Stockton, Manitou, Ironwood, and Cat Islands. Somebody at the research station had told them it must've broken loose. The senior chief said that happens about once a year, accusing non-nautical college students who don't know how to properly tie the boats to the dock. Viper said that after the storm he'll go back and see if there's any kind of accountability for who had what boat."

"How much do you want to bet that boat was assigned to Ms. Frantz?"

"Sucker bet." Keene yawned. "No worries. We'll have

a boat to come get you, but please understand, it might be a day, maybe two."

Ali's eyes met his at Keene's bad news. "It's okay." Her jaw started to quiver. "Just don't let the kidnappers take me again."

Heath darted out of his seat and pulled Ali out of her chair and into his arms.

"I've got you. You're safe now with me." He rubbed his hand up and down her shaking back. This was a familiar routine with most rescued women. The mere thought of being taken again, held against their will, scared them to their bones.

"Pitbull, is everything okay?" At the sound of his nickname, he realized he was still connected to Gramps.

He held the phone to his ear. "We're fine." He glanced at his watch since it was right in front of his face. It was nearly eight o'clock. "Consider this my last check-in until morning. Team bravo out."

"Roger that. Local base, out."

Heath looked down at the woman in his arms who had stopped shaking. He reached down and lifted her chin so he could check her beautiful brown eyes. Red from the tears but no signs of shock. "I'm not going to complain if you want me to stand here and hold you, but we don't have any way of reheating your gumbo and you seemed to be enjoying it so very much. If you eat the rest of your supper, I'll have a surprise for you."

Her face morphed right in front of him. The frightened kidnapped victim was gone, and the strong, resilient woman was back. "I don't know. Tempting. But I'm actually pretty comfortable where I am. I'm not a child you have to tease to finish a meal. When I'm ready, I'll eat every drop, even if it's cold. Just tell me what surprise you have for me, and I'll decide if it's better than what I already have right here."

The male part of Heath didn't want to tell her because she might decide to leave his embrace. The professional rescuer in him was already shaking his head, telling him that holding her was wrong and he should tell her immediately as he stepped back. If he didn't let go of her soon, he might lower his head a few inches until his lips touched hers.

"So, what's it going to be?" Her words were a husky whisper.

He compromised with the warring parties in his head. He smiled. "How do you feel about warm chocolate cake?"

Ali grimaced. "Hard decision."

It was Heath's turn to grimace at her choice of words. If she were to remain in his arms, she'd soon learn the meaning of hard. He was only a man. True, at his age should be able to control his more basic body functions, but Ali Frantz was a very appealing woman.

She glanced over to the table before returning her gaze back to him. "Although I really want to stay in your arms —because I feel safe for the first time in what feels like weeks, maybe even months—I really want to eat that gumbo while it's hot." She smiled up at him and something warm washed through his body. "Besides, I truly believe that if I needed another hug, you'd give it to me." With her arm still around him, she took a small step backward. "Thank you. I needed that and I appreciate you taking the incentive and moving…because I wouldn't have asked for it."

He wanted to lower his head and kiss her even more now. "Anytime. You don't have to ask me. I'm always happy to hold you."

"I'll keep that in mind." She gave him a little grin and stepped out of his embrace. They both sat back down and hurriedly finished their suppers before they got cold.

"I know this is biodegradable, but do you have a sealable garbage bag?" Ali held up her completely empty bowl. "Everything has to be bear-proofed."

He held up a two-gallon sturdy sealable bag. "Leave no trace is even more important on a rescue mission if we are being tracked by bad guys with guns. I have more of these if we need them." He opened the bag and held it out to her.

As soon as she dropped her gumbo bowl into the bag, she looked up at him expectantly. "I believe you mentioned chocolate cake. I haven't had dessert in days. That's how I could tell my kidnappers were men."

Chuckling, he asked, "Why is that?"

"A woman would have packed something chocolate in the lunches they left me. It might only be a candy bar, but it would've been sweet." She stood very close watching him pull the small chocolate cake out of the bag he'd used to heat her meal. "That entire system is fascinating. Was it warm enough to heat the cake after it cooked my meal?"

He picked up the bag and held it up to her. "Stick your hand inside. There's still a little residual heat. If we're working in the snow, we often stick our hands inside to warm them up because we tend to eat without gloves."

"Amazing. This would make a wonderful in-classroom experiment." Her smile grew. "There are all kinds of educational applications from thermodynamics to chemistry. The bonus would be that the students get to eat the food. I think I'll work on this idea."

She took her small piece of cake and sat down. As soon as she dug her spoon in, she yelped in surprise.

Laughing, Heath told her, "Yes. The frosting is on the inside. If you're lucky, it tastes more like hot fudge cake."

She looked over at his dessert. "What is that you are eating?"

"A warm butterscotch cookie with caramel drizzled on it." He gave her a sheepish smile. "I'm not a fan of chocolate. Offer me something strawberry or caramel and I'll be first in line."

"I like strawberries, too." She grinned devilishly. "Strawberry daiquiris are my favorite way to enjoy the fruit. Made with spiced rum is my absolute favorite." She looked at him with questions in her eyes. "Do you drink?"

He decided to tease her. "Of course. Sports drinks, water, not big on sodas." Her face took on a definitely worried look, so he decided to answer the question she didn't ask. "I really enjoy a good bourbon. I like it either way, neat or on the rocks." He chuckled. "I don't drink those fruity drinks. Offer me a cold beer and I'll never turn it down, unless I'm working. My favorites are dark craft beers like a porter or a Dunkel. Some stouts are a little too heavy for my taste."

"I like a cold beer on hot day." She stared down at her empty bowl, only thin lines of chocolate left where her spoon scraped the rest.

"Go ahead. Lick the bowl. You know you want to," Heath teased.

Her eyes met his and held. "Meredith Frantz would have a heart attack if I did that." Her grin was fiendish once again. "So don't tell her." She held up the bowl and a pretty pink tongue came out of her mouth and licked the edges.

Heath's brain automatically wondered how talented she was with that tongue. What it would feel like dueling with his. How it would torture his erect cock. He immediately stood and took his dessert packet to the garbage bag, hoping desperately that he could talk down his erection before she finished licking every drop of chocolate from the small bowl. He started cleaning up the cabin, collecting all the trash from their meal for disposal.

Everything in the large duffel bags was laid out in a specific order. The next section was the head. Normally they set up the latrine on the outer edges of camp. He stared at the camouflage pop-up tent and automatically glanced up at the windows. Given the intensity of the winds, there was no way in hell it was going to survive outdoors.

Heath glanced around the hut and found what he considered the emptiest corner. It was also the farthest away from the beds. The cabin's designer did an excellent job with space utilization. He could also tell that it was a work in progress.

He took out the fifteen-by-fifteen-inch square bag that contained everything from the toilet to the tent. All the men were thrilled that it weighed less than two pounds. An invaluable find by Xena who claimed the entire world was a man's bathroom, but their rescued female victims needed something more discreet…and so did she.

"I'm going to set the bathroom up over here. It would never survive outdoors in the storm," he explained but was sure she understood his reasoning. It took him longer to unzip the bag than to pop the tent open. The toilet Xena had chosen had two sides and a seat. He cursed trying to hook the specially made chemical bag onto the corners before he flipped down the seat. He jiggled it, testing its stability. It was amazingly stable.

He looked at his handiwork with satisfaction and realized that Ali was standing right beside him.

"That thing's amazing." She looked into the duffel bag. "Feminine products. You guys have thought of everything."

He shrugged. "Most of the time we're rescuing women. Having Xena on our missions has made us one of the best in the world." He reached into the privy kit and handed Ali a squirt canister the size of a lipstick tube. "This stuff works wonders. If you haven't used it before, put two squirts in the bag before you have to poop. When you're finished, lift the lid and everything fits inside the silver bag." He demonstrated the proper folding and sealing. "Then put it with the other trash."

"I'm so glad you set this up so I can test it…now." She stepped into the tent and zipped the door closed then immediately unzipped and stepped back out. "I know you have toilet paper in there somewhere. I don't care what you're supposed to do with it once it's used, but I'm putting it in the bag."

She was so damn cute. "Works for me."

She repeated the process and a few seconds later yelled through the thin tent, "Relieving oneself is a biological function. Every person does it from the moment of birth until death. Same with passing gas. And burping. I truly appreciate the privacy of the tent, though. As you saw in that other place, there was no privacy. On the other hand, there was no need for privacy. I was there all alone." Much quieter, she added, "For four fucking days."

Heath wasn't sure if her monologue was to cover the noises she made while in the head or if it was a girl thing, talking to each other while in the bathroom. Either way, she was cute. She came out with the sealed silver bag and headed straight to the large garbage bag. She went directly to the correct duffel and got another bag.

He quickly grabbed it. "I'll take care of that since I need to use it." He also grabbed another one he'd used to replace his. "Here's a toothbrush kit and a bottle of water. Spit back into the bag. They're supposed to be disposable toothbrushes but since we might be here for a couple days, you'd better keep it. I have a tube of toothpaste so no need to conserve what little bit they give you."

"Oh, look. There's even a little container of floss." She looked at him with accusation in her eyes. "Did you rob a dentist?"

"No need." Before he could get out another word, she jumped in.

"Let me guess, Serena buys them by the boxful."

Grinning, he nodded. "You got it."

"Then are we going to bed?" Ali asked innocently.

CHAPTER 9

As soon as the words were out of her mouth, Ali realized what she'd said. "I meant, are we going to bed in our own beds?" Was she the only one with a dirty mind? She could feel the heat rising up her neck and into her cheeks.

Then she looked at Heath.

His grin said that his mind went to the exact same place.

"I'm just going to go over here and brush my teeth." Ali waggled the toothbrush kit bag, turned her back to Heath, and walked away a few steps. She set everything down on the counter that she figured the owners used for washing dishes. At the zip of the bathroom door, she slid a glance in that direction and let out a deep breath.

She didn't mean to be teasing. It was just her smart mouth. Her father considered it her quick wit. Her principal sometimes failed to see her humor. Mostly, her students got it.

Ali never would have thought she'd get so much pleasure from brushing her teeth. Four long days had gone by without her mouth being scrubbed with a toothbrush, so she brushed twice. She considered going for a third time, but Heath had already finished in the bathroom and with his teeth.

"We'll just sleep in our clothes," he announced as he went to his bed and lay down. "I'll leave the light on for you."

Ali crawled on top of her sleeping bag and covered herself with the space blanket. A moan escaped as she stretched out. She giggled and flopped her left leg and arm up and down.

"Feels good, doesn't it?" his low voice rumbled across the cabin.

"You have no idea." Just being able to lie flat and position her body any way she wanted reinforced her feeling of freedom.

"Actually, I do. I was chained while I was a POW in Ethiopia. That feeling of being able to move your limbs once again is glorious." She could hear it in his voice. He did know.

Ali tried to sleep on her back, then rolled to her left side. She was facing the center of the cabin and it didn't feel right. She rolled to her right. With the wall inches from her face, she studied the grain of the wood then closed her eyes. Inhaling deeply, she let it out very slowly. Normally, this relaxed her brain, and she'd fall asleep easily. No luck. She tried lying on her back again to no avail. The room was just too damn bright.

For the last four days her body was keyed to the sunrise and the brightness of the cabin. With the bright light, she felt as though she needed to be getting up rather than going to bed.

"Heath, are you still awake?" she whispered.

"Yes."

"I really hate to complain because you've been so wonderful, but can you turn off the light, please? It's just, I can't seem to go to sleep with all this light." She made her voice sound as pleasant as possible.

Ali watched him get out of his bed and walk to the lantern in the middle of the room. "Usually kidnap victims are afraid of the dark after we rescued them, so we always keep the light on." He dug in the bag for a moment. "How about we compromise." He turned down the intensity of the light and placed it in the bathroom. The thin tent walls were illuminated from the inside, shining enough light to see her way around the cabin.

He stepped out and said, "This way we have a little light and finding the bathroom in the night will be easy."

"It's perfect." It gave her just enough light, but it wasn't as bright as it was before.

Heath handed her a small penlight. "This will be easier to handle than the huge flashlight you'd used earlier."

"Thank you." She saw that it had a few unusual buttons on it, so course she pressed each one. There was a red one, which, of course, turned the light red. Same with the blue. She twisted the end and the beam got wider. "You might not get this back."

"Keep it." He chuckled as he crawled back into his bed.

Ali couldn't quiet her mind. Heath had said her father had sent them. What demand had the kidnappers made of her father? Would he have done it? Money? Something else? She had this mental discussion with herself several times over the past four days. While alone in the cabin, there was no one to give her answers.

Now there was.

"Heath, are you asleep?" she whispered.

"No." He rolled to his side facing her. "What's on your mind that's keeping you from sleep?"

"I know you said you were just one member of the team, but do you have any idea what demand they made of my father?" Her voice was nowhere near as strong as she'd like it to be. She was obviously more upset about this than she'd thought.

Without hesitation, he spoke. "Your kidnapper knew your father was about to go into a committee meeting when he called. He wanted your father to support raises for park rangers."

"That was it?" She sat up on the edge of the bed. "Some douchebag was willing to kidnap me just to get my dad to support something in a committee?"

Heath mirrored her position. "Yes. Your father recorded the conversation and shared that with our team."

"How did Dad know he had me?" She wasn't sure she wanted to know the answer to that question.

"The kidnappers used your phone to send your father a video of you chained to the floor." Heath continued, "A few minutes later he called, again using your phone, making his demand."

She could only imagine what her father had seen. Worse, what he had feared. "I should have told your teammate to tell them that nothing bad had happened to me. I hadn't been beaten or raped."

Her eyes met his in the barely lit room. "I forgot to tell

them that. I'm sure they're worried sick about it. Especially Mom. I'm a terrible daughter."

His bottom lifted off the bed, but he sat right back down. "Your physical condition was in my initial report. I'm sure they've been told. Our policy is to contact the parents as soon as we've located the victim. It's also our policy not to let the victim talk to the parents until we have them someplace safe and secure. Even though this cabin is dry, and I am armed, you're not considered secure until you are at our local base. In this case, until we get you to the hotel in Bayfield. We'd also feel better if the kidnappers had been captured or otherwise dealt with."

"I understand." And she did. She knew it could be a possibility that whoever took her would end up dead.

Heath smiled. "As soon as we have you back to our base, you'll have an opportunity to shower, eat some good food, before we take you to Duluth. Someone, usually Xena, will fly with you back to D.C. and deliver you to your parents' door."

"No, they won't." Ali straightened her back. "I'm not leaving. I'm only a few weeks into my summer semester. Once I finish this research, I'll have enough credits for my second master's degree. Besides," her shoulders slumped, "if I go back to Washington, Mom will have an entire list of men for me. I hate first dates. I fucking hate D.C. parties."

"Why would your mother have a list of men for you?" Heath leaned back against the wall.

Ali let out a long breath. She hadn't told any of her friends about this, not that she had any real tight girlfriends, so why was she telling her rescuer? She had no idea, but he seemed easy to talk to.

"I'm thirty-three years old. Shortly after I turned thirty, my mother got tired of waiting for me to find a husband. Not just any husband," she waggled her index finger as though she were talking to students. "Oh, no. The *right* husband who will help enhance my father's run for presidency. She doesn't give a shit, at least not anymore, about what I want in a husband. And if I go back home, Mom and Dad are going to want me back in their house, not my condo. They are going to be so scared that I'll get kidnapped again."

"So, what's wrong with all the men your mother is choosing?" He covered up with the blanket.

She was getting chilled and mirrored his position, blanket and all, except she pulled her legs onto the bed. "Politics. That's what I hate about parties. Everybody just stands around and talks about politics. None of the men I've dated had ever been camping. Not even one had ever caught a fish, cleaned it, or cooked it over an open fire for breakfast. Most thought that was gross. One took me sailing for our first date. I thought he'd be a possibility until we were out on Chesapeake Bay, and he couldn't figure out how to get us back to Annapolis where he'd rented the boat. I sailed the boat back by myself. I have lots more first date disaster stories."

"I might want to hear some of those tomorrow." He grinned. "It's going to be a long rainy day." He cocked his head. "You've been an adult for quite a while. Don't you think your parents would understand you wanting to stay to finish what you've started?"

She shook her head. "Not my mother. She wasn't at all happy that I took this position." She changed her voice to just sound like her mother. "How do you expect to find a

79

suitable husband on a remote island in the middle of Lake Superior?" She changed her voice back to her own. "She was even less happy with me when I told her I'd be having a great time up here *doing* the things I love, not *looking* for love."

"Have you found anyone that sparked your interest?" His question had multiple meanings and she suddenly understood.

"No. There is no jilted lover here. At least not for me. There are only two men who have been here longer than me, Howard and Cliff. I don't even know their last names. They're an interesting pair. I'd say they're both loners that have been forced to work together. They don't talk much even to each other. They've been here since May and will stay until the end of September for their bear research. It might be a multi-year project since Howard is working on his PhD. Although I've spent time with them, I don't know what Cliff is doing."

"There are no other men?"

"We had a couple young men, I think they were going to be seniors this fall, but they were only here for two weeks. Complaining the entire time." The last sentence was said under her breath.

"City boys?" he asked with a chuckle in his voice.

"Most definitely. And Momma's boys." She grinned at the memory. "As the oldest woman at the research camp, I pointed out how to them on day two how neat and tidy everyone else kept their bunks and personal belongings. When it was still a mess on day three, they found all their shit out in the front yard. When they returned from their daily duties they started bitching. I handed them a tent."

She giggled before she continued. "Then they really

started complaining. I told them, *you can live like an adult, or you can live out in a tent by yourselves anyway you want.* The smart mouth one then said," she changed her voice, "*what am I supposed to do with this?*" Ali shook her head. "They finally confessed that they didn't know how to even set up a tent. Since it was getting dark, I gave them one more chance, and specific instructions as to what was expected. By the end of their two weeks, I think the two frat boys had grown up a little." She stifled a yawn.

"You ready to lie back down and try sleeping again?"

She nodded. "Good night, Heath." She stretched out on top of the sleeping bag and tucked the space blanket tight around her, the way her grandfather would do while they were camping. She breathed in deeply and let it out slowly. By the second time, she was asleep but not before she heard Heath say good night.

CHAPTER 10

HEATH'S INTERNAL CLOCK HAD HIM AWAKE BEFORE DAWN. Of course, he woke up with a morning hard-on. At his age, it wasn't unusual, nor was it an every morning event. What surprised him was that he'd never had an erection during a rescue. If it happened while he was at home, he'd simply take care of it during his morning shower. Taking care of it in the corner tent bathroom wasn't an option either. Nor was stepping outside under the guise of taking a leak. He'd established a three-hundred-and-sixty-degree safety circle covered by cameras and he was sure that whoever was on duty at the ops center both locally and at Holt Agency didn't want to watch him jerking off. For all of ten seconds, he considered exercising but didn't want Ali to have to put up with his stinky body in the small cabin until someone from his team was able to pick them up.

He did need to go the bathroom, so he decided to take care of that first. The darkness in the cabin would hide his erection and hopefully he could talk it down by the time he was done using the facilities. As quietly as he could, he slid from the narrow bed and padded on silent feet to the bathroom. Thankfully, when he emerged, silver bag in hand, his erection was gone. He crawled back into bed, wondering what the hell they were going to do all day while the storm raged on.

As the cabin was slowly illuminated by the morning light filtering through the gray rain clouds, Heath crawled out of bed once again and straightened the sleeping bag and pulled the blanket as tight as possible before opening breakfast and heat packs. Their morning meal was ready about the same time the interior of the cabin was fully lit. He poured himself a cup of coffee and sifted through the bags for something to do...as in something to keep his mind off the pretty high-value target.

Yahtzee.

Heath had found a small waterproof bag with dice, stubby pencils, and game sheets. A deck of well-worn playing cards as well as a stack of scratch paper they often used for tic-tac-toe with rescued younger victims were also inside.

"Mmm. Something smells good." Ali's hoarse voice came from the area of her bed. She was curled up in a ball with her head completely covered by the blanket. Crinkling noises were followed by her head emerging, like a turtle under a silver shell. "Please tell me there's coffee."

He considered teasing her then thought better of it. She didn't seem to be a morning person. "There's coffee." He poured her a cup and took it to her bedside. "You're going to want to sit up to drink this." He handed her the cup as soon as she was upright.

She breathed in the coffee then smiled. "I hope you taste as good as you smell."

Heath stared at her over his shoulder. *She didn't say what I thought she said?* All kinds of ideas ran through his mind as to how they could occupy the long hours of the rainy day tasting each other. There were condoms in those bags. They were supposed to be used to cover the open end of the weapon barrel if it was going to get wet, but they were condoms.

He watched her sip the coffee. A slow smile spread across her face. "You taste even better than you smell." She took another sip as Heath's sexual plans curled away with the coffee steam.

"Yes, it is damn good coffee," he agreed. "Breakfast is also ready. Do you want to eat in bed or at the table?"

She immediately stood and shucked off her blanket, striding to the table. She set down her coffee cup in front of the same chair she'd taken the night before. "I'll be right back." She pointed to the head then quickly disappeared inside.

Heath brought the food and silverware to the table then refilled his coffee cup. Just as he was sitting down, she joined him.

"Hot food again? This is wonderful. I can't thank you enough, Heath. If you'll let me, I'll cook lunch." She smiled at him before eating a bite of scrambled eggs and cheese.

He smiled back. "Deal. As soon as we finish our breakfast, I need to check in."

Ali glanced at the daylight outside the windows. A long string of cheese dripped from her shaking fork. "Did...did they come?"

He reached across the table and put his big hand over her free one. "I won't know until I check in." He gave her trembling hand a light squeeze. "Would you feel better if I call them now?"

Without a word, her head jerked up and down.

He patted her hand before he lifted his and got up to retrieve the satellite phone.

Heath put it on speaker in the middle of the table so Ali could hear as it started to ring. "Bravo team checking in. I have you on speaker as Ali and I eat breakfast." He didn't wait for Gramps or Viper to answer. "Did you see any activity at the other hut?"

"Well, good morning to you, too, Pitbull." Viper was in sarcastically rare form that morning.

"Ali is a little anxious about any activity last night." His eyes met hers and he could see the fear in them.

"No. Nothing entered the cabin or opened the door but depending on where they've hunkered down in the storm, they might not have been able to get there. Unless they're camping on Outer Island, unregistered, it would be nearly impossible for them to reach that cabin, or yours." Viper obviously sipped coffee. "According to the Coast Guard chief, who I paid a visit to about an hour ago, he said the lake recorded waves over fifteen feet tall last night. He also told me that some idiot local kids were out there surfing this morning."

"Gramps mentioned last night that the chief had told him there were three families camping here on Outer Island. Is there any chance we can find out who they are and run them?" The possibility that her kidnappers might be camping on the island had Ali's entire body shaking.

He pulled her into his lap and held her close to his chest. Whispering in her ear, he told her, "You're safe with

85

me. I've got you." He slowly stroked his hand up and down her back.

"Five steps ahead of you," Viper bragged. "Before I took over for Gramps around one in the morning, he'd already run them. A local photographer and his wife, who have visited the island multiple times over the last five years. Two families with a total of five children are in the other two tents. The husbands own a roofing company together, one wife has a bookkeeping company, and the other works on a tour boat that guides people around the islands. None of them have any relationship to a park ranger. Out of boredom in the middle of the night, I took a deeper dive on all of them and came up with zilch."

"Any chance of another thermal satellite picture today?" Heath was sure Ajax had already asked.

"Supposedly, they were going to try. It seems this storm is quite thick, and they couldn't guarantee anything."

"Understandable." Only through their connections with the vice president were they even able to request such an expensive endeavor, say nothing about it being granted. He wanted to change the subject. "What's the weather forecast?"

"Do you have windows in there?"

Both he and Ali looked up near the ceiling where they could see out. "Yes."

"Look outside. More of the same for approximately twenty-four hours." Kenner could be heard sipping more coffee. "The chief said that when they get one of these in the wintertime, it could last a week dumping several feet of snow. Last year it snowed for a hundred and forty-five days. They had almost a hundred inches of the white shit.

That's nowhere near what we used to get in Alaska, but fucking snow is snow."

"That's one of the possible effects of the Great Lakes warming; increased snowfall." Ali had spoken loud enough for Kenner to hear.

"Really?" both men said at the same time.

She nodded. "That's what my research is all about, water temperatures here in Lake Superior."

"Hey, I gotta go. Looks like Ryker and Xena are up. They're calling in. Local base out."

Viper was gone so Heath ended the call on his end.

He rubbed his hand up and down Ali's back. Her breathing had evened out. "Feeling better?"

She nodded her head but didn't say anything.

Heath loved the feel of her in his arms, her head snuggled into his chest. He didn't care if she ever moved. For a minute, he wondered if she'd fallen asleep. Her breathing had slowed to long even breaths. In. And out. In. And out. She took a deep breath as though to fill her lungs.

"Heath." She lifted her head and looked at him. "Although I'd love to stay right where I am, I haven't had a hot breakfast in five days, and I don't want that one to go to waste." She slid off his lap and he let her.

She positioned herself across the table from him and resumed eating her cheesy eggs. "Maybe it's because I'm so hungry for food other than cold-cut sandwiches and fruit, but these are damn good eggs."

"Yes. We've had four years to decide which are the best lightweight meals," he explained. "These eggs are one of my favorites, so I always bring them."

They were soon done and had disposed of their dishes in the filling garbage.

Ali flapped her arms out to her sides, and she looked around the cabin. "So, what are we going to do with an entire day?" She glanced down where the food pouches were stored in his duffel bags. "Besides prepare lunch and supper?"

Heath grinned. "Have you ever played Yahtzee?"

"You cheat. You already had threes filled," Ali laughed and accused him seven hours later. They were back to Yahtzee after playing several rounds of hearts, spades, poker, and a cutthroat game of go fish. She'd made lunch with very little direction. Then the games resumed with tic-tac-toe, hangman, a ridiculous game of Pictionary followed by charades where Ali had rolled on the floor laughing so hard at Heath, tears rolled down her cheeks.

"I certainly did not cheat." He held up his card inches from her nose. "See. It's not like we have erasers. There's only one set of numbers in that block." He smiled at her insistence. "This means I win again. I think we've had enough of this game, now." He collected the cards and dice then slid them back into the bag.

Ali crossed her arms over her chest and crossed her legs. She over-dramatically pretended to glare at Heath. "How come you're so damn good at all these games?"

"In the Navy, you spend a hell of a lot of time killing time. You can't take whole boardgames with you into the field but cards, dice, scrap paper, they don't weigh much." When he put the games away, he moved to the food section. "Are you hungry? We can go ahead and start supper now if you'd like. These are bigger meals and take a few extra minutes."

She came up behind him and leaned over, her hand on his shoulder, her face inches from his. As she leaned down, her breasts brushed across his arm. "I think I'd like this one. Is it any good?"

Bent over, she turned and held up the bag. Heath couldn't see anything except her face. They'd had so much fun that day. He couldn't remember laughing that much in his life. He'd never spent such an enjoyable day with a woman. This rescue was so opposite of every rescue he'd ever been on, and there had been hundreds between the Holt Agency and while in the SEALs.

"You can have anything you want." He meant the double entendre as he stared into her beautiful brown eyes. He was no longer in the Navy, so he wasn't bound by military rules. They were consenting adults.

But his honor wouldn't let him take advantage of her state of mind. Twenty-four hours ago, she was chained to a pole in the middle of a similar hut. She was the job. As he'd been told in the very beginning of the Holt Agency, you don't fuck the job.

"I'm sorry." Heath stood and pulled her up with him. "I shouldn't have said that, at least not that way."

She slid her arms around his neck. His hands automatically went to her hips. "You can have anything you want, too."

He saw the lust in her eyes. Her offer made blood rush to his cock. He rocked back a fraction of an inch so she couldn't feel his growing erection. "Ali, you're a very beautiful woman. Under other circumstances, we'd be on my bed right now. But you've been through a very traumatic event. It's not uncommon for women we rescue to get a little hero worship for us."

Hurt flashed through her eyes before understanding settled there. She finally gave several small nods then stepped back. He immediately felt the chill. She was gone and so was her body heat.

"Of course, you're right. It must be a delayed reaction to the adrenalin." Ali stared out the windows. "Sex is one of the most natural reactions after long-term heightened emotions. That's all it was, adrenalin letdown."

Heath wasn't sure who she was trying to convince, herself or him. Because he wasn't going to analyze his reaction to her, he kneeled next to the big duffle bag and held up multiple choices for supper.

Their intense moment disregarded; Ali joined him. "I think I want this one tonight." She picked up one of the heat bags and began assembling her own, so he began making his.

"I know you learned a lot about camping and survival in the SEALs, but did you camp as a child?" she asked as she got a bottle of water for each of them.

Heath grinned. "You mentioned camping with your grandfather. I also camped with mine. The family still has a fishing hut on the mainland just outside the Redcliff reservation." He glanced around their current abode. "In some ways, it's like this except much older. Pawpaw built the bunkbeds when my two uncles were young. My cousin and I were barely old enough to hold a fishing pole the first time they brought us. I spent most of my summers, until I started working, with Pawpaw and Mamaw. That also meant I spent a great deal of time with my uncles and cousins who lived in this area."

"I'll bet you know how to clean fish, too. Am I right?"

He chuckled. "Damn straight." He smiled at the memory. "My cousin Robbie and I used to have competitions to see who could clean the most fish. Pawpaw had a rocker at the cabin, and he'd sit there with a beer in one hand and an old stopwatch in the other. My uncles would make sure we each had the same amount of fish and same sizes."

"Who won?" Ali asked with her elbows on the table and her head in her hands.

Still smiling, he replied, "Depended what day it was." He looked at her before asking, "Did you ever go ice fishing?"

She gave a visible shiver. "Once. That was more than enough. Did you cook over open fires?"

"Hell, yes." He slowly shook his head side to side. "While the adults set up camp, it was mine and Robbie's job to collect firewood." He checked his watch for the cooking time. "Supper is almost ready. Did you pull out a dessert?"

"No, damn it. I forgot." She grinned. "My brain was fogged with post-adrenalin sex thoughts." She got up and wandered over to the bag and called out all the desserts, pulling two of them.

They were able to finish supper before it got too dark. Preparing for bed, though, was done by lantern light.

Heath couldn't go to bed before she did, but he was emotionally drained.

Ali yawned as she used the wet wipes to clean her face and hands. "Would you mind if I call it an early night?"

He smiled. "I was hoping you'd say that."

"It's weird, isn't it? How rainy days seem to make you tired. All you want to do is sleep." She smiled back at him. "Thank you for making the day go very quickly...even though you cheated," she teased as she crawled into her bed.

Heath called in to local base ops one last time for that day. He moved the lantern into the bathroom and made sure there was plenty of toilet paper and replacement bags. As he crawled into his own bed, he considered this might be his last night alone with Ali. If the weather report was to be believed, his team would be picking them up tomorrow.

His last thought was that he didn't want his time with her to stop.

Partially awake, Heath heard the wind pick up as though the storm had to kick the great Lake Superior one last time on its way east.

He fell into a deep sleep.

Crash.

The door flew open and banged against the wall.

Heath was instantly awake, his gun in his hand pointed at the open door.

Ali sat up staring at the outside, limbs and leaves blowing past the doorway, some being shoved into their tidy cabin.

She screamed.

The door bounced against the wall each time the wind surged.

With slightly bent knees, eyes down the barrel of his pistol, he prowled through the shadows to the open door. Stepping out barefoot into the storm, gun forward, powerful flashlight searching their surroundings, he turned to reenter the cabin. As he stepped in, he almost tripped over an eighteen-inch log. Running his flashlight over the door, he saw where it had hit just above the handle.

He let out a long slow breath as he kicked the storm debris out and closed the door. His flashlight immediately went to Ali. Curled in a tiny ball sitting on her bed, wrapped in her blanket, her whole body shook.

He strode across the small floor, grabbing the phone on the way, and sat beside her, sliding his arm over her shoulders. "I've got you. You're safe. Did you see the log that hit the door at the handle and opened it?"

With small jerks of her head side to side, she squeaked out, "No."

He quickly dialed local base ops. It rang three times before Viper answered the phone. "This is bravo team. Check the cameras starting five minutes ago. Our door flew open."

"On it now. Checking your perimeter first. Fuck, Pitbull. It looks like you're having a hurricane out there. Going back five now." His friend was quiet as he held Ali, rubbing her back. "It looks like a tree fell down and exploded. Huge pieces were picked up by the wind and thrown at your hut. Only a fucking idiot would be out walking around in that shit." He laughed then. "Maybe we need to change your nickname to fucking idiot. I'm watching video of you walking around outside in the pouring rain with all kinds of debris flying around. Okay, now you're back inside safe and sound. You were the only human I saw walking around out there."

"Thanks, man. Hopefully I can get her back to sleep."

"Breakdown?" Pity laced Viper's voice.

"Maybe. Team bravo out." Heath hit the end button before even hearing *Ops out*.

He held her for a long time before her breath calmed down. "You ready to go back to sleep?"

Terrified eyes met his. "Heath, can I sleep with you?"

"Sure." He was an idiot. A fool of the biggest kind.

He picked her up, blanket and all, and carried her to his twin-sized bed. She immediately crawled over and faced the wall. He put both blankets over them, rolled to his side, and put an arm around her waist.

Ali was crying.

94

CHAPTER 11

THE MINUTE HEATH PICKED HER UP, SHE KNEW SHE WAS going to break. She could feel her strength shattering, one fractured chip at a time. As her mother had taught her, she'd suppressed her fear and soldiered on…with a smile. She'd kept it buried all day, locked tight in a vault that she could ignore, as they played ridiculous games without either of them knowing how close she was to falling apart. When he laid her down on his bed, it smelled like him. His strength and masculinity oozed from the sleeping bag mattress.

She was safe.

Heath was strong. She no longer had to be the strongest one.

He would never let her fall to a kidnapping again. Secure in his arms, she purged the tears filled with fear and the loneliness of four days in the kidnapper's cabin. Ali had no idea how long he'd held her, rubbed his large powerful hand tenderly from the top of her head down her arm and repeated it time and time again while he whispered soothing words to her. "I've got you now. You're safe. I'm here and I'm going to protect you." She cried herself to sleep.

Ali woke to complete silence and shadows caused by the lantern in the bathroom tent. She must've rolled over in the middle of the night because she was facing Heath, tucked into his broad chest. Listening carefully, she heard...nothing...except Heath's steady breathing and slow heartbeat. For the first time since they'd entered that cabin, it was quiet.

"The storm passed about an hour ago," Heath grumbled and pulled her in tighter. "Go back to sleep. We've got another couple hours before we're expected to check in."

"I'm sorry...about...this. If you want me to move, I'll go back to my own bed now." Not that she really wanted to leave. He was big, and warm, and she felt protected in his bed.

"I like you right there." He kissed the top of her head. "Go back to sleep. Going to be a big day tomorrow."

"Don't you mean today?" she sassed.

"No. As far as I'm concerned, it's not tomorrow until I wake up," Heath mumbled.

"But you're awake now."

"No, I'm not. I'm still sleeping." His big hand rubbed the length of her backbone and pushed her head into his chest. "And you should be too. Now, go back to sleep." She felt his lips on the crown of her head, the protective way you would a child.

She scowled at the thought of him treating her like a child. She was a grown woman. Embarrassed because she'd acted like a small child who'd been sent to her room on a sunny Saturday, grounded, not allowed to play with her friends. Sulking and feeling sorry for herself. Bad things happen to people every day. She should be thankful that she was alive and that her father had sent Heath to rescue her. She needed to suck it up, lift her chin, and square her shoulders. She was a Frantz.

Fuck. That sounded just like something her mother would say.

What she really needed to do was go back to sleep. Heath was right. Tomorrow—no, today was going to be eventful. She listened to his steady breathing and found herself matching him as he inhaled and slowly exhaled.

Ali must've fallen back asleep because when she awoke the next time, relatively refreshed, daylight was streaming through the windows. She was lying on her back taking up most of the bed. Heath was on his side, his left arm angled so his hand could hold his head. His free hand gently brushed stray strands of brown hair from her face, running his fingers through her hair, softly touching the outer shell of her ear.

"Good morning. Feel like coffee and eggs?" His gruff morning voice vibrated her libido awake. Would he always be this gentle and accommodating first thing in the morning?

What the hell was she thinking? Heath thought of her as a child, not a woman who wanted to wake up every morning with the man at her side who touched her tenderly all over before sliding into her, giving them both an incredibly good morning.

"Okay." She inhaled a deep breath through her nose and let it out slowly to get her heart pumping blood to her fingers and toes. Because her nostrils were filled with the smell of man, Heath in particular, she repeated the process. "Give me a minute, and I'll get up and cook."

"Too late." He rolled off the hard bed. "Breakfast will be ready in five minutes so if you hurry, by the time you're done with your morning routine, breakfast will be ready." He glanced over his shoulder at her. "You're really a heavy sleeper."

She stirred in the bed, stretching from her toes to her fingertips like she did every morning. "I wouldn't know. I've never slept with me." She sat up and made her brain work. "I don't think I've slept with anyone else in the same room since my roommate in college...until I came here. The research facility has kind of a coed bunkhouse. At least we have separate bathrooms and showers."

His expression was shocked when he looked at her. "No long-term boyfriends?"

Shaking her head, she got out of bed. "I told you, I'm an expert at first dates. If I choose to take a man to my bed, he doesn't spend the night." At the shock on his face, she told him bluntly, "Women have needs, too. My battery-operated boyfriend gets the job done but there's nothing better than a man's hands and fingers, especially if he knows what to do with them." On that note, she zipped the door to the modicum of privacy allowed in the tent bathroom. Damn, she must be horny. In the weeks that she'd been there, the only times she'd been able to use her dildo was on her day off while staying in town. It had been nearly two weeks since she'd had a day off.

Once again, Heath phoned in while they were eating breakfast, leaving the phone on the table with the speakerphone.

"This is team bravo checking in. You are on speaker-phone as Ali and I eat breakfast."

"Good morning, bravo team. The storm passed a couple hours ago and looking out the window, the lake is like glass. The small craft warning has been dropped. Satellite was able to get a thermal picture after the storm. Analysts in Washington are still reviewing it, but we expect to receive a picture within the hour. Xena and Ryker are on their way to pick you up. They should be within comm reach now. I'll see you when you get here. Local base out."

Heath went to the small bag he'd carried as his back-pack and dug in the side pocket. He removed a small case about the size of a ring box and opened it. He screwed what looked to be very small earbuds into one ear then returned to his breakfast.

"Team bravo online. Team alpha come in." He repeated the call a few times before he smiled. Someone must have answered.

Because all communication was in his ear, it was a one-sided conversation for Ali. Fortunately, he gave her a running commentary. "Xena is talking to me, and I hear Ryker driving the boat." He pointed to the phone and hit a few buttons. "The satellite will identify our location and relay it to team alpha."

He gulped down the last few bites of his breakfast then said, "Ali, we need to be ready to leave within five minutes. I want to meet them downstream at the lake if at all possible."

She ate a few last bites then quickly threw away her meal packages into the large garbage bag. She knew how to break down camp. Gathering their sleeping bags, she stuffed them back into the satchels, compressing them down as small as she could get them. She folded the blankets while he tore down the bathroom tent and folded the toilet, sliding them both back into their proper bag before storing them in the huge duffels.

Glancing around, she didn't see a trace of anything they'd left. She sat down at the door and put on a clean dry pair of socks he had just handed her. Next came the bags, then the waterproof pants, and finally she Velcroed her feet into the slip-on shoes. She slid on her jacket and was ready to go.

"I can carry something," she announced.

Heath handed her the backpack that he'd worn when he first showed up at the kidnap cabin. He grabbed the huge duffel bags and threw one over each shoulder after he had his boots on.

"Let's go." He opened the door, and she followed him out, securely shutting it. Heath hooked a new padlock on the door, leaving the key in the lock. "Leaving the cabin. Walking to the lake." He must've been talking to the other team.

Walking through the slippery woods was slow going. The ground was saturated. A few times he talked to the other people. They were about halfway back when he swore under his breath. "Fuck!" He probably didn't want her to hear but she did.

"What's wrong?" Ali asked.

"We need to hurry. There's a boat tied up about fifteen hundred feet down the lake."

Ice shot through her veins. She couldn't make her feet move. "Is...is it them?"

"Ali, we have to move faster in case it is. Ryker turned

off the boat quite a way back and they drifted in further south. From their position they can't see the other boat so they figure it can't see them either. But that means we have further to go." He put his arm around her, and they started to move.

Once they reached the shore, they ran south until they saw the rescue boat. A stunning tall blonde stood on shore. "Pitbull. Throw me the bags and you help her get on board."

Heath did as ordered and the bags were on board before Ali was able to sit down. The woman pushed the boat away from shore and leaped onto the bow, rapidly making her way to the driver who hit the gas. They sped away at full speed. She took the phone from the man and immediately started talking.

"I'll make introductions once were farther away from here." Heath pulled her to his side. It felt so good having his arm around her, simply him touching her, once again.

When the woman hung up, she came to the back and sat on her heels in front of them so they could hear her over the roar of the motor.

"Hi. I'm Xena." She had a warm smile as she extended her hand. "You must be Ali. May I see the wrist and ankle where you were bound?"

Ali held out her wrist. Xena was very gentle as she unwrapped it and carefully examined the bruises.

She gave Heath a quick smile before returning her gaze to Ali. "He did a very good job tending to your abrasions. Let's go ahead and leave the wraps off them now." Xena looked down at Ali's makeshift boots. She then glanced up at Heath. "We need to add Ziploc bags to the list."

He grinned back at her. "I already did."

Xena's face turned grim. "I'm sorry we had to hurry you along but we're now confident that the other boat belongs to your captors. The camera left in the first hut recorded someone in a mask and hoodie, wearing gloves, entering the cabin carrying a cooler. He picked up the handcuffs and threw them against a wall before picking up the other cooler and leaving. We have experts in Washington looking at the footage. Hopefully, they'll find something that can help us identify him." Xena grabbed Ali's knee and gave it a small squeeze. "You're safe. All three of us are highly trained for these circumstances. We'll have you back in Bayfield in about an hour. We have a room for you at the same B&B where we're staying. You'll be able to take a shower and change into your clean clothes before your parents arrive."

"My parents are here?" Fuck. "What the hell are they doing here?"

Puzzlement crossed Xena's face. "They're here to take you back to Washington."

Ali folded her arms over her chest. "They made a long trip for nothing. I'm not leaving."

Xena slid a glance to Heath who nodded. "She wants to stay here and finish her research."

Xena pasted on a smile. "That's between you and your parents. Once we hand you over to them, we're officially done unless your parents want us to find the kidnappers."

"I'll talk to them." Ali tried to sound polite. She sure as hell would talk to her parents. She was staying right there in the Apostle Islands.

An hour and a half later Ali regretfully stepped out of a steaming shower. She'd stood under the water scrubbing then re-scrubbing, trying to finally feel clean. Feeling guilty, knowing others like Heath may need to shower also, she finally turned off the hot water. It was wonderful that she could put back on her own clothes. Thankfully, someone from their team had gone to Stockton Island and gathered some of her clothes. Clean underwear felt glorious.

As soon as she'd had been shown to her room and the door was closed, she'd stripped off all her kidnap clothes and thrown them in the garbage with glee. Had they taken her back to the research center, she would have burned them.

They were all going to meet in a conference room down the hall for a debrief and a hot lunch. When asked what she wanted to eat, she'd mentioned a place two blocks away that served locally caught fish sandwiches made with the best tartar sauce she'd ever eaten. Secretly, it was the French fries she wanted even more. She needed the crisp fries, a food her mother despised, to fortify her defiance. Her mother would be there all too soon.

CHAPTER 12

THE ROOM PHONE RANG AS EVERYONE WAS CLEANING UP after lunch. As team leader, Ryker answered. After a few words, he hung up and turned to Ali. "I'm heading down to the lobby to meet your parents. I'll bring them up to this room. Do you want us to stay? Or leave?"

She squared her shoulders and lifted her chin. "I don't care if you hear what I have to say to them. I am staying here in the Apostle Islands to finish my research and my next master's degree."

Xena walked to her and put her hand on Ali's forearm. "Your kidnappers haven't been caught. That could be very dangerous for you. You might be safer back in Washington."

Ali shrugged. "I've worked too hard for this. I'm not giving up now. If there's some crazy person out there wanting to kidnap me, he can do it in Washington as easily as he can here. Probably easier. There's a lot fewer suspects in this area than D.C." She swung her gaze to Ryker. "Now that I'm rescued, are you going to notify the local or state police? The FBI? I don't even know who you notify in a case like this."

"The FBI." Ryker held her gaze. "That's up to your parents. They were the ones who were threatened by the kidnappers." He moved toward the door. "I'm not going to leave them standing in the lobby any longer. Someone might recognize them. Your father doesn't need this to show up on social media."

Heath watched Ali shred a leftover napkin in her lap until he couldn't stand it anymore. He approached her cautiously. "If you want me to, I can stay right here. Sometimes dealing with parents, especially as adult children, can be tough."

When she reached over and touched his forearm, heat ran up his arm and circulated his whole body, seemingly kicking his stomach and groin at the same time. "Would you mind staying close to me? After all the time we've spent together since you rescued me, you feel like my only friend here."

He put his free hand over hers. "I'll be glad to stay here with you as long as you need me."

This was already the strangest rescue he'd ever done, but for her to say he was her only friend there punched him in the heart. She thought she was going to need support, so he'd be there for her.

When the senator and his wife walked into the room, it was her father who practically ran to her and swept her into his arms. "Oh, baby girl." He held her tight against him as they swayed. "I'm so glad they found you. And fast." Emotion ran through every one of the senator's words, his voice cracking. The man had his eyes squeezed tight. Heath was sure there were tears from both Ali and her dad.

He glanced over to her mother who stood just inside the door, both hands clutched to the handles of her designer purse. She wore a demure light blue dress with navy low-heeled pumps. Although she'd traveled several hours that day, her hair and makeup looked perfect. Her face was tightly drawn as though to hold in all emotion as she viewed the affection between her husband and daughter.

As the senator and Ali separated, he quietly instructed her, "Go say hello to your mother. She's been very worried."

Stiffly, Ali walked across the room to greet her mother with a hug that didn't go much beyond her mother's shoulders and a kiss on the cheek. Meredith Frantz grasped one shoulder of her daughter's and leaned in, keeping the purse between them like a barrier.

Heath wondered what kind of cold bitch would treat her daughter like a stranger. He wondered if perhaps Ali was a stepdaughter, birthed by an earlier wife of the senator. Not that it was any of his business because their job was done. They had rescued the senator's daughter.

"Are you ready to go?" her mother asked. "We have a plane waiting in Duluth." Her mother scraped her gaze from Ali's still damp hair to her scuffed boots. "I'll call and have Carol meet us at the airport with something appropriate for you to wear."

Heath watched as Ali inhaled deeply and let it out slowly. She straightened her back and squared her shoulders. "That won't be necessary, Mother. I'm not going home with you."

Internally, Heath smiled. *That's my girl.*

But she wasn't his anything. Except the job. Maybe now that the job was completed, and he was going to stick around and take some vacation, he might see her.

"Don't be ridiculous." Her mother matched Ali's pose. "You've been through a major trauma. I already have an appointment for you with Dr. Crane in two days. He comes highly recommended to deal with posttraumatic stress syndrome." Her eyes darted around the room, and she moved in closer and spoke just above a whisper. "Now, Annali, you're creating a scene."

Ali's head jerked back as though she'd been hit. "No, Mother, you are. I'm sorry you went to all that bother to come here, but I'm staying and completing my research. I've been an adult for nearly half my life. I am the one who makes decisions about my life. I choose to stay here."

"Jonah, talk some sense into your daughter." Her mother huffed and stepped aside as her father joined the discussion.

He lifted a hand and affectionately touched Ali's face. It must've been a familiar move because she leaned her cheek into his palm. "My precious baby girl, the kidnapper is still out there. You might still be in danger. Please consider coming home with us."

"I know the kidnapper is still out there, Dad. Are you now going to involve the FBI?" Ali stared at her father.

He finally shook his head. "No. You've been rescued, and that's the most important thing. You're free of those…" his whole body cringed before he choked out, "chains." He swallowed hard. "Bringing in the FBI now is only going to draw attention to your kidnapping. I'd rather we keep this quiet." The senator looked at each member of the Holt Agency.

His gaze stopped at Ryker. "You guaranteed that no one other than your team would know about this."

"Yes, sir." Ryker spoke with confidence. "People in town may speculate, but I can guarantee you no one on my team has leaked your daughter's kidnapping. This is far from our first rescue of a high-profile family member. We are professionals. Now, if you wish, we can put a team on site and attempt to find the kidnapper."

Her father threw an arm around Ali. "I know this research means a lot to you."

"Oh, Dad, it really does. Not just for my master's, but I made a commitment to the university. It's too late in the summer for them to find someone to replace me. My data gets combined with water temperatures and water content from all over the Great Lakes. This is a massive and important research that deals directly with climate change."

Jonah Frantz looked directly at Ryker. "The vice president told me that your agency also provides bodyguards. How soon can you have a team here?"

Ryker looked at Heath and Kenner. Both men gave a barely perceptible nod. "I have two men here now."

"I want Heath." Ali stepped forward as though to interject herself into the men's conversation. "He saved me from that awful place. He stayed with me all during the storm and took good care of me. He fed me well and protected me." She then looked at him and shyly added, "If you're available."

He smiled at her. "I already consented." He wanted the

opportunity to be close to her. The problem was, she was still the job.

Her father's gaze returned to Ryker. "I want the fucker caught who had the audacity to take my girl and chain her to a pole. When you find him, we'll turn him over to the FBI. I have a few connections there who can keep this quiet."

"Sir, we can't guarantee we'll find the kidnappers. They may have come into the area specifically to take her and have already left. We'll do our best to track them down." Ryker looked at Heath and Kenner. "In the meantime, we will keep your daughter safe."

"Do it." The senator extended his hand to each member of the Holt team, thanking each one. When he came to Heath, he stopped. "I can't thank you enough. I know it took this whole team, and then some." He pulled his daughter to his side and gave her a one-armed hug. "It sounds like you went above and beyond. 'Thank you' are such small words for the appreciation I feel. I owe you my deepest gratitude."

In a shocking move, her father pulled Heath into a strong embrace. He whispered into his ear, "Take care of my girl."

Still hugging, Heath whispered back, "I will."

When they separated, he pulled his daughter into his arms for one last hug. Heath couldn't hear the quiet words that were exchanged before they parted.

The senator walked over to his wife. "Meredith and I want you to know how much we appreciate everything you did and how quickly you found our daughter." He gave her a broad smile. "We know how bad storms can get on the Great Lakes. When you get back home, precious girl, you're going to have to tell me about camping on Lake Superior."

Ali ran to her father and gave him one last hug. "Love you, Dad."

"Love you, too." He then kissed the top of her head.

"Goodbye, Mother. I'll see you both when I return the week before school starts." She stepped over and leaned in then gave her mother another kiss on the cheek.

"Sir, ma'am, I'll walk you out." Ryker stepped to the door and followed them out.

Ali immediately walked to Heath. "Looks like you're not going to get rid of me anytime soon." He wanted to wrap his arms around her and simply hold her again, but he couldn't. Although the situation had changed, she was still the job.

She dropped her head on his chest. "I could sure use a drink. I don't care what time it is."

"We'll all join you," Ryker said as he stepped back into the conference room that had been their local operations center. He opened a cabinet that turned out to be a wet bar. "The company is buying. What are we drinking to celebrate a successful mission and a new contract? Ali, pick your poison."

Still in front of Heath, she lifted her head with a smile. "Let's go have a drink."

CHAPTER 13

"ARE YOU ALL RIGHT? THE QUESTIONING GOT PRETTY intense yesterday afternoon," Heath asked Ali as they loaded the boat to take her back to Stockton Island. He volunteered to take the first round of bodyguard duty, claiming that she would most likely feel more comfortable with him to start. He didn't care if he was right or not. He was going to be the one to figure out the best way to protect her.

"I'm fine. It wasn't bad at all. I want these guys found as much as you do. Probably even more." Ali stood on the dock and handed Heath his small backpack. "That's everything. Kenner, if you're ready to go, I'll grab the lines while Heath gets all this gear stowed."

"I'm more than ready to get this show on the road." He glanced around the Bayfield marina. "I guess in this case, I should say that I'm ready to get this show on the water."

Heath caught the lines and Ali jumped onto the boat with the ease and grace of someone who'd done it all her life. He liked that she was comfortable on the water. So was he. He wondered if she scuba dived. That made him wonder what she looked like in a bathing suit. His eyes followed her feminine curves currently hidden under loose-fitting clothes. Come to think of it, that's all he'd seen her in.

"Where to, Mademoiselle? Your water chariot awaits," Kenner asked Ali as he putted out into the marina's no-wake zone.

"The research center on Stockton Island, please. Do you know where that is?"

"Yes. I went to the research center to ask questions just before the storm. Then I went back to get your clothes while you two were on your way into Bayfield with Xena and Ryker." Kenner shook his head side to side. "Weird bunch out there. Nobody seems to know who's in charge."

Ali giggled. "That's because no one person is technically in charge. Most students are working on different projects for different professors. The University of Michigan received the grant that I work on, but all my findings go to professors at the Great Lakes Research Center, which is part of Michigan Tech. Two young men who were up here a few weeks ago had a small grant through the University of Minnesota. I think Howard's bear research is through a small university somewhere in Wisconsin, but his PhD will be conferred through University of Michigan. So, as you can see, no one is really in charge of the research station. The facilities are technically owned by the National Park Service."

"I met the camp cook, but he was clueless," Kenner replied.

Ali laughed. "You're right. Keeping track of students isn't his job. Feeding those students three meals a day seven days a week is his job. About every ten days a woman from the mainland comes out and she cooks for us for a couple days while Ed gets drunk down in Ashland."

"Who coordinates where everybody sleeps?" Heath was curious as to how the whole system worked and who he'd have to speak with if Ali needed different sleeping arrangements.

"Nobody." Ali shrugged. "When new people show up, whoever is there tells them to grab an empty bunk and points out the bathrooms. If there's a problem, we tell Ranger Roy. Roy Stevens," she clarified. "He's responsible for the buildings and the grounds."

Heath and Kenner exchanged a glance. The kidnapper wanted Senator Frantz to increase pay for national park employees.

"You called him Ranger Roy. I take it he's a national park ranger?" Heath asked.

"Yes. He's also in charge of the Stockton Island Visitor Center but there are other rangers over there all the time. I've heard him complain about the campground at the northern end of the island. He claimed they're an even bigger pain in the ass than we are."

It took nearly an hour to get to the research center. As Heath and Kenner tied the boat to the dock, they noticed all the other boats with the word research in capital letters down the sides.

"Ali, were you driving one of these when you were taken?" Heath asked.

"I have no idea." She stood on the dock staring at the other boats. "I'm sorry, but I don't remember anything about my kidnapping. I could have been taken in my sleep, or anywhere out there. Like I told all of you yesterday, my research involves all the islands. Every day I go out in one of these boats, I take water temperatures and samples at various depths. Sometimes I help other students if they need to go to the same area or islands where I'm testing that day, so we share a boat. I can't trust my memory. I can't tell if I'm remembering that day or three weeks before then."

When Heath heard her voice break, he immediately went to her and pulled her into his arms. He didn't care if Kenner saw him do it. She needed it and he refused to deny her a simple hug.

The tour of the camp took all of two minutes. It consisted of a state-of-the-art lab where Ali, and a few long-term students, had their own designated section. Other areas were shared by students. Beside the lab was a long barracks-style building with a set of bunks followed by a set of lockers followed by another set of bunk beds and two more lockers, repeated down both sides. The men's shower and bathroom were at one end and matching women's facilities were at the other end.

While Ali put away her clothes, Heath turned to Kenner. "No fucking way is she safe in here. It's wide open, yet I can guarantee nobody sees anything. Nor would they say anything. Not that there's anyone in authority to say anything to. We have to figure out a better way."

"Totally agree. Try to talk her into staying permanently at the B&B." Kenner shook his head. "This isn't going to work."

Heath stood close to her and spoke quietly. "Ali, this is too open. We can't keep you safe in this environment."

Heath held her gaze. "You're going to have to come back and stay at the B&B in Bayfield."

She glanced at him over her shoulder. "No." She then returned to her unpacking.

What the hell? What happened to the woman who agreed with everything and followed orders immediately?

He decided to try again with a different approach. "Ali, we've been assigned to protect you." He swung his arm wide. "We can't do that here. You're completely exposed. Anybody could step in that door and shoot you. One tiny drop of the right drug in your food when you're distracted by someone else living here and someone could carry you off while everybody else sleeps. Please, be reasonable."

She turned her whole body toward him and placed her hands on her hips. "You be reasonable. The lab is here, the boats are here, and even though it isn't the best food in the world, the program pays for it. Besides, the truth is, the food isn't half bad. If I were on the mainland, I would have to pay for my own food. I'm on a teacher's salary. You have any idea how little I make? Also, I would lose an hour or more every day starting from there rather than here. Sometimes I work in the lab until after midnight. I'd have to take the boat back to the mainland, which would be another hour. I would lose so much sleep." She lightly touched his forearm and he wanted to melt as heat rushed through him. "Heath, I need to be here."

He really did understand her point of view and her needs. "Let me see what I can figure out."

"Stay here with her," Heath ordered Kenner. "I'm going out to look around."

"Are you checking out that small building on the side?" Kenner asked.

"Yes." Heath had noticed a small version of the bunkhouse around the side. It only took a minute to pick the lock. As he stepped in, he thought he'd try the light switch before digging out his penlight. To his surprise, the lights worked. The room was relatively empty. It had a few cots, at least twenty years old, certainly not meant for men the size of Heath and Kenner. Well-built dressers and small closets stood between the beds.

"What the fuck are you doing in here?" a gruff voice came from the doorway. "You kids know this building is off limits. It's got a real big sign right out front."

Heath spun around to find a man wearing a national park ranger uniform with its buttons stretched to the limit over his very round belly. His belt was lost somewhere underneath. His pants seem to fit and his boots were sturdy and scuffed.

"Sir, do you know what they use this building for?"

"*I* use it for storage. Now, young man, I've answered your question. Answer mine. What are you doing in here?" The ranger crossed his beefy arms over his chest, making his belly sag even lower.

Heath thought about it for a minute then decided to tell the truth. "I'm looking for a safe place for Annali Frantz and her security contingent to stay."

The park ranger dropped his arms and took a few steps further into the building. "Is Miss Ali in danger?" He looked around as though someone were hiding behind the boxes either listening or ready to attack.

Heath regretted his choice of words, but they were out there now. "I'm not at liberty to discuss the matter with you."

"She's one of the nicest people who have ever been

here. She doesn't hesitate to put those newbies in their place. Smart, too. She's always helping the other students." The ranger stepped in closer to Heath and said above a whisper, "I know who her father is. Are you Secret Service? Has he announced his run for president?"

"No, sir. We are not Secret Service and to the best of my knowledge, Senator Frantz has not announced his intent to run for president. We've been assigned to Ms. Frantz as security detail." He needed to redirect this conversation. "Now, back to this building. What's its purpose? And who exactly are you?"

All smiles now with his arm extended, the man moved to Heath. "I'm National Park Ranger Roy Stevens. Welcome to my island. Everything that happens, and doesn't happen, on this island is my responsibility."

He looked around the building they were standing in. "Back in the days when they didn't want boys and girls sleeping in the same room, this was the girl's dorm." He grinned hugely. "It still has running water. All I need to do is turn it on." His eyebrows pinched together. "We might need to run the water for a while. I'm sure the pipes are rusty."

"How's the roof?" Heath was now seriously considering this aged building.

Roy scoffed. "Probably better than the one on the new bunkhouse. This was built back in the day when materials were meant to last and made of real wood." He maneuvered his large body in front of Heath. "I can get on the horn right now and get our springtime cleaning crew out here to clean this place up spick-and-span within about two days. Will that be enough time for you?"

Heath didn't answer. "Can these beds be taken out and

put in storage? They're a bit small for us. We'll bring in some cots and our own bedding." He looked into the other man's eyes. "I'm putting you on notice that I will be installing cameras. Most likely you won't even notice them. There won't be any holes, so you needn't concern yourself with that. They'll come down when we leave. We have a boat for her to use. She and her detail will be taking meals in the dining facility."

He stepped into Ranger Roy's personal space and looked down at the man, who was a good eight inches shorter. "People on the mainland don't need to know anything about these arrangements. You seem to like Ali. You don't want to put her in danger, do you, Roy?"

"No. I like Miss Ali. I'd hate for something to happen to her." The middle-aged man was shaking his head violently. "No. I won't tell anyone." He swallowed hard. "But the students might talk."

Heath showed him two rows of straight white teeth. "No, they won't." He stepped back. "Turn on the water and clean the lines. Part of that is going to happen as your cleaning crew scrubs this place top to bottom. I know your budgets are stretched thin and we wouldn't want to take anything away from important improvements. Have your cleaning crew leave me the bill and I will get them paid immediately. I'll give you forty-eight hours before we need this move-in ready." He handed the ranger a card. "You run into difficulties, or need us, call this number."

Heath walked out of the building and back to Ali and Kenner in the bunkhouse. "Our facilities will be ready in forty-eight hours. I'm sorry, Ali, but for the next two days we need you to stay at the B&B with our team."

She inhaled a deep breath through her nose and out

slowly through her mouth with a dramatic sigh. "I guess I can suffer with clean white sheets and a soft bed, not to forget the hot showers, for the next two days." She glanced at her locker. "When we come back from my sample gathering and temperature testing, I'll grab some clothes after I finish in the lab. Gentlemen, I need to pick up my equipment from the lab and then I'll be ready to go to work."

CHAPTER 14

"I'LL ONLY BE A FEW MINUTES, GUYS. I WANT TO CHECK my workstation." The feeling of home swept through Ali the minute she stepped back into the lab. Even in college, she preferred to be in the lab than in the classroom. Labs were also her favorite classes to teach. More than once she'd considered leaving the students for pure research. Her time in the Apostle Islands seemed to push her in that direction.

True to her word, she'd checked her area to be sure nothing had been moved or been tampered with, gathered her testing equipment, and was ready to leave in under five minutes.

"May I take any of that out for you to the boat?" Heath offered.

She smiled up at him. "Thanks, but no. I'm used to carrying it. I like to keep everything in a certain order so when I reach for it, I grab the right thing."

They were in the boat and ready to cast off when a young brunette with bouncy curls called out as she trotted across the large lawn toward the dock. "Hey, Ali, are you going anywhere near York Island?"

"Tell her no," Heath ordered in a low voice so as not to be heard by the young woman.

But Ali was going that way. She needed to go all the way to Sand Island today, the next one past York, then up to Devils Island.

His eyes softened. "I'll explain once we're on the water."

"Sorry, Britt. I'm not going to York Island today." She didn't lie. She wasn't going to York. "Check with Davey. I think he said he was going to Raspberry this morning."

The young lady smiled and waved. "Thanks, Ali. I'll go ask him. You're the best."

Kenner was back at the boat controls again this morning, so Heath got the lines.

"I could get used to this kind of service," Ali told the two men in the boat. "Normally I'm out here wrangling lines and pushing off the dock by myself."

"From now on, Ali, you will never be alone." Kenner looked at Heath. "One of us will always be with you."

"The bathroom stall is certainly going to be tight," she quipped.

Both men laughed, as she'd intended.

"In all seriousness, other students will no longer be allowed to go out in the boat with you," Heath explained. "There are too many possibilities for things to go wrong. If by some bizarre circumstance they were able to overcome your bodyguard, that would leave you alone with your kidnapper and twenty-one islands. He wouldn't make the same mistakes twice. Do you understand?"

Waking up alone, chained to that pole, day after day.

Not knowing why they'd left me there. "I'll do anything you need me to do." She grasped Heath's hand and squeezed tight. "Just." She swallowed hard. "Don't let them take me again."

Heath wrapped his strong arms around her and pulled her to him, holding her head to his chest. "You're safe with me. And when Kenner is guarding you. We've got you." She felt his warm lips on the crown of her head.

"Where to, Ali?" Kenner asked as he passed the no-wake zone buoy, breaking the spell between Ali and Heath.

She stepped back. "I need to go to Sand Island, but I don't want Britt to see me out that way." She checked her chart then smiled. "Kenner, have you ever been to Devils Island?"

He smiled as he glanced at her. "Are we headed to hell? Or to French Guiana?"

Ali looked at Heath who just grinned back at her. "Neither, and you're in for a treat. Devils Island, Wisconsin is very unique. Would you like me to take the wheel so you can sit back and relax? It's going to take a long time to get there, like two hours. More to where I need my samples."

"I've got this. Just point and give me directions." She guided Kenner between Manitou and Ironwood Islands, then between Rocky and Otter Islands, past Bear Island before heading over the two and a half miles of open water before reaching the northernmost Apostle Island known as Devils Island.

"These caves are beautiful," Kenner noted.

"Slow down," Ali insisted. "Go in closer. Look how clear the water is. It is very deceptive. This is much deeper than you imagine."

"How deep?" Kenner asked.

"Way over your head."

Kenner looked to Heath for confirmation.

"It certainly is. I learned to scuba dive in this lake. Because it's so clear and pure, you can see so much at deep depths. On average, you can see twenty-seven feet down into the water. And that's average across the whole lake."

"No fucking way." Kenner looked between Heath and Ali.

Ali gave him an evil grin. "Do you want us to throw you in the water and see for yourself? The surface water temperature has warmed up to forty-six degrees Fahrenheit. Because the water is so clean, it actually warms at subsurface depths quicker and retains the warmth longer. A sunny summer will warm the lake deeper so when the cold Arctic winds blow across the warm lake, the winds pick up more water than average and it thusly becomes a snowy winter in Buffalo, New York."

"Really?" Heath asked.

"Really." She checked the GPS. "We're almost to the coordinates for my first samples." She showed Kenner the coordinates and he slowed to neutral.

After she'd collected and stored her samples, Ali recorded her data. She then gave Kenner the next coordinates before sitting down beside Heath.

"Did you know that Devils Island may be the only location in North America with naturally growing heath rush?" She loved sharing tidbits of information, especially since this one carried his name.

"I had no idea." Heath grinned at her. "I also have no fucking idea what the hell heath rush is."

She leaned to the side and bumped his shoulder with hers. "It's a grass. Don't get excited, it's not natural to this area. They're pretty sure it came to the island on an army surplus bulldozer the National Park Service purchased. It was brought here to make trails on Devils Island. The grass is actually native to Iceland and parts of Europe but was introduced to Greenland, where the bulldozer had been, as well as Tasmania and New Zealand. Whatever the reason, it's here now. You may know it as goose corn or mosquito rush. I'm going to continue to call it heath rush and think of you every time I come to Devils Island."

"We're here," called Kenner from behind the wheel.

Over the next two hours as they circled Devils Island, Ali sampled and recorded data. After the third repositioning, she could tell the men were getting bored. Maybe she could engage them a little more.

"Why do you think they called this Devils Island?" she asked.

"Because it's so far out here in the middle of nothing that only the devil would want to live here?" Kenner suggested.

Heath squinted his eyes at her. "I think the Indians actually named it, didn't they?"

"Good job." She applauded. "Give that man a gold star for the day. Yes. The Indians called it Evil Spirit Island. During storms, big waves slap into these caves and it sounds like thunder booming. I can't attest to that being true because I've never been on this island during a storm. After the one we just went through, I think I'll be going to one of the B&Bs during the next storm." She reached over and touched Heath's arm. "Although I appreciate every single morsel of food you fed me, especially the hot meals, I think I'd rather have real home-cooked meals with fresh vegetables."

"I'm right there with you." He looked directly at her as he said those words. She could imagine the two of them in one of the old B&Bs, snuggled in a bed together as the storm raged around them. She would be safe in his arms.

"Time for the next samples," Ali announced.

"Oh, joy." Kenner unenthusiastically asked for the next coordinates.

By the tenth stop, Ali was driving the boat because men were asleep, stretched out on the side benches in the sun.

On her next repositioning, Heath woke up.

"Some bodyguard you are," she dramatically chastised.

"Nobody lives on Devils Island. Nobody can even get onto it anymore because storms last winter destroyed the dock. The information was confirmed by both the National Park Service and the Coast Guard." Heath moved in closer to her. "So there, Miss Smarty-pants."

"How did you know my panties are smart?" She loved to tease him.

Heath closed his eyes and seemed to grit his teeth. She was getting to him. Good. That proved that she affected him just as much as he affected her. He wouldn't touch her when they were stranded in the cabin but now that he was no longer rescuing her but protecting her, she might convince him to do more than verbally banter.

When he opened his eyes, he changed the subject. "How many more at this island?"

"I have one more position to sample before we head to

Sand Island. That's a long haul south so we'll eat our lunch before we leave."

"Thank Christ. I'm starving." He dug into the cooler they'd brought with food and drinks. She had a separate one, temperature controlled, for water samples. "Ham and Swiss or turkey and some kind of white cheese?"

"That's provolone but I'll grab mine when I finish this island's samples. You go ahead and eat if you want, though." She glanced over at the still-sleeping Kenner. "You might want to wake him up so he can pick his sandwich and extras."

She stood at the helm and put the boat in gear, keeping a careful eye on her GPS to be sure she was in the proper location. They had traveled five hundred feet farther down the island. By the time she took her samples and logged in the data, she was quite hungry.

Facing the two men, she said, "This is one of my favorite islands because its geography is so unique. The base of the island is sandstone, a sedimentary rock that is basically sand that was laid in layers over six hundred and sixty million years ago while all this area was underwater. Several ice ages in this region have carved out the islands then wind, ice, and water sculpted these caves. I think the caves are simply beautiful. So many colors and the way they reflect in the water. It's gorgeous."

She looked at the two men and couldn't tell if they were interested or bored. "I'm sorry. It's the schoolteacher in me who loves science. Sometimes I forget that not everybody wants to know why. Or how."

"No, no, Ali. It's all very interesting. I spent summers here for years and had no idea why this specific area is like it is." Heath looked a little embarrassed. Then his stomach growled.

"I'm so sorry. Let's eat." Ali grabbed her sandwich and sat down at the helm behind the wheel. "What I often do is put the boat into the lowest gear and eat while I cruise past the caves."

"Sounds good to me." Kenner took out his phone and started taking pictures between bites.

Fifteen minutes later, they headed southwest past the western edge of the Apostle Islands toward Sand Island. "It will take us another hour to get there so if you men would like to sleep, go right ahead. Nobody is going to get to meet out here."

"Thanks, but I'm good." Kenner came to the seat across from the helm. "This place is amazing. The only time I've ever been on any of the Great Lakes was during boot camp on Lake Michigan north of Chicago and it didn't look anything like this."

"Did you have lakes while growing up?" she asked.

"I was born and raised in Alaska. We have millions of lakes and lots of water… when it isn't frozen. That's why I got the hell out of there just as soon as I turned eighteen and joined the Navy. They promised to send me places that were warm. I've been to the Middle East several times and different places, Africa, South and Central America, but this is my first time up in this area."

Embarrassed because she went into super teacher mode earlier, she decided to ask, "Would you like to know more about Lake Superior?"

"Sure."

Heath moved into the seat behind hers. "I want to hear this."

"If you've heard enough, don't hesitate to tell me to stop. Like I said, I'm a teacher by trade and I love sharing science and nature."

"Go ahead, please." Kenner turned so he faced her a little more.

"Okay, just remember that you asked for it." Now, where to start? "First, this lake alone has ten percent of the planet's fresh surface water. We have more water in the aquifers under most of the United States that run from a couple feet deep to three thousand feet below the surface. The volume of surface water is why Lake Superior is so important. Then there's the lake's use for transportation. Ninety percent of the U.S. iron ore production is mined in Minnesota and Michigan and most of it is carried on ships through the Great Lakes."

She was in open water, so she turned her head to see if Kenner and Heath had glazed over or fallen asleep.

"This is interesting. Keep going," Kenner encouraged.

"Okay. Speaking of ships, there have been about three hundred and fifty recorded shipwrecks on Lake Superior with over ten thousand lives lost. You've probably heard the big lake doesn't give up its dead. That's because it's so damn cold. You're both sailors so you should understand this easily. Normally, after a few days in the water, enzymes in a dead body make it bloat and float. But when a ship sinks in Lake Superior, it can go down over a thousand feet where the temperature is close to thirty-two degrees Fahrenheit. Just above freezing. The enzymes don't work down there."

She had their attention so she kept going. "Have you ever heard of the Edmund Fitzgerald? There's a song about it sinking."

Both men nodded.

"Dad and I met a man who actually dove on the Fitzgerald. It sits in five hundred and thirty feet of water on the Canadian side. He told us that the bodies were completely intact. He said it was the spookiest place he ever dove." Ali shivered at the thought.

"I read someplace that you can't dive on that site." Kenner sat on the edge of his seat.

"You can't anymore without permission from the Canadian government. Back in two thousand six the families of the sailors who went down with the ship got the Canadian government to declare it sacrosanct."

"The deepest I've ever been was two hundred seventy-five feet. Even then the mix gets pretty rich, and your time on the bottom is so limited," Kenner said.

Heath grinned. "I've been to eight thousand feet...in a submarine. A few of us were on board when they did some pressure tests in the Puerto Rican trench."

Kenner swatted Heath on the shoulder. "Showoff."

Ali pulled up to her first sampling site off Sand Island.

"Are you bored yet?" she asked the men.

"The ride here went pretty fast," Heath admitted. "I love listening to your stories."

She giggled. "Good, because you're probably getting to hear a lot of them over the next few days." Or weeks. She prayed it didn't go longer than a month.

CHAPTER 15

"I'LL CHECK IN AT NINE, TWELVE, THREE, SIX, AND BEFORE we go to bed. Then again first thing in the morning," Heath informed Ryker, Xena, and Kenner. They were now the Wisconsin delegation of Ali's security team. Keene had gone home to the Holt Agency base back in Indiana to be with his wife, Kelly, and recently adopted son, Jock.

"I'll be out in five days to rotate with you. If you need anything in the meantime, just call." Xena packed her day bag. She and Kenner were going back to the kidnap cabin to retrieve the camera, chain, and hardware, hoping for fingerprints or something traceable to the kidnappers. The kidnappers hadn't been back there since the day Ali was brought to Bayfield. Ryker was going to man the Bayfield base and as the co-owner, deal with agency business.

"If you come up with anything at all that I can tell Ali, please call me. She's putting on a very good front, but I think deep down she's scared of being kidnapped again." Heath waved goodbye to his team and went down the hall to her room.

"Ali, do you have everything?" he asked as he picked up her small bag sitting at the door.

"I didn't bring much over with me. You said we were only going to be here another two nights, so I brought two changes of clothes." She looked at him and smiled. "Ready to go to work?"

"Let's go."

Thirty minutes later they were at the lab gathering her equipment and lunch for the two of them. They took a few minutes to pop in next door and check out their newly cleaned sleeping facilities.

Heath looked around with a critical eye. The old beds were gone, and their new cots had been delivered along with fresh linen that would be provided weekly by the laundromat in town. Xena would bring a clean set with her when she came out. Ranger Roy had taken it upon himself to create a wall between the two beds using the closets. Whoever was on duty could hear Ali if they were needed yet each had their own personal space. The cots were arranged so that each had a small bedside table. That would be a perfect place for his gun. They would share the bathroom, but they had during the time spent in the rescue fishing cabin.

"This will be nice." Ali sat down on one of the cots and ran her hand over the bedding. "In the bunkhouse, there's always somebody who snores and I'm usually a light sleeper." Her gaze went to Heath. "I noticed that you don't snore. Do the other bodyguards?"

He shrugged. "I have no idea about Xena, but I can assure you that Kenner does not."

Ali rose and walked into the bathroom. "Look at this. Someone put up pretty green curtains and green rugs in front of the sinks and shower. They don't have these niceties in the bunkhouse." She turned on the water and watched it run clear for a few seconds. With a huge smile she threw her arms in the air and twirled. "And we have all this space to ourselves."

Inwardly Heath smiled. She looked like a joyous child. He was well aware she was all woman. Now, with just the two of them alone in this separate building, she was going to be an even greater temptation. But she was still the job and off limits.

"Where are we going today?" he asked as they left their new sleeping quarters.

"The southern islands for the next few days. It will take us all day today to do Madeline Island."

It was nearly suppertime when Heath and Ali headed back to the research center on the northwest side of Stockton Island.

As they neared shore, Ali looked worried.

"What's wrong?" he asked.

"We never discussed how we're going to explain you to the students. They're going to ask questions as soon as we sit down to supper."

"The entire Holt Agency had a discussion about this very issue last night. We've decided honesty was the best approach. At supper, I want you to introduce me as Heath, one of your security detail. Use only first names. If we must, we'll mention our security agency is in Indiana. Mostly, we'll do that to avoid the question if we are Secret Service. We will never impersonate any other agency or claim to be affiliated with the government." He touched her shoulder. "Are you okay with this?"

She nodded. "I guess I have to be. I liked just being

Ali, a high school biology teacher from Virginia. Everyone will treat me differently as soon as they find out that my father is a senator. It won't take them long, either, to discover that he's considering running for president. Then shit really changes."

She let out a long breath. "Part of the reason I took this position here, so far from social media and television, was to get away from all of that. I guess they were going to find out sometime. Might as well be today."

Heath maneuvered the boat to the dock and with Ali's help, secured it for the night. He followed her to the lab where she dropped off the day's samples.

In typical Ali method, she straightened her back and squared her shoulders then held his gaze. "If you're ready, let's do this."

They followed the line through the buffet then found two seats side by side. As soon as everyone was seated, Ali stood up. "Most of you know me, but for those who don't, I'm Ali Frantz. I'm here for the entire summer semester. Some of you may recognize my last name. Yes, I am the daughter of Senator Jonah Frantz. No, even I don't know if he's going to run for president. But as my father, he is worried about me since I'm out here in the middle of bum fuck nowhere. He has insisted that I have a security detail now."

She smiled and pointed to him. "This is Heath. He's my bodyguard for a few more days."

He carefully watched the eyes and expressions of each of the students. Possibly one of them had kidnapped her or at least knew something about her kidnapping. He made a few mental notes as he gave everyone a chin lift.

"There will be other bodyguards," she continued. "One

of the other changes is that my security detail and I will be living in the small building on the other side of the lab. No one is allowed in our new quarters." She smiled. "Tomorrow morning, I intend to move all the rest of my stuff out of my bunk in here. That should give everybody a little more room."

"I claim her bunk," a young man with long sun-bleached hair down to his shoulders immediately shouted.

"Okay, Danny claimed my bunk." She swung her gaze to him. "But you can't have it until tomorrow even though I'll be sleeping in the other building starting tonight."

"No problem, Ali. Good things are worth waiting for." He flashed bright white teeth before he resumed eating.

As they sat down, Ali said quietly so only Heath heard, "I was one of the first students here for this summer and claimed the best bunk. Howard and Cliff have damn good ones also because they were here even before me. Unfortunately for them, they'll be here until early September when the National Park Service closes most of its facilities."

A cute redhead stood up and announced, "For those of you who don't know me, I'm Jane. I'm here working on a NOAA grant, that's weather, but I wanted to tell you something exciting. Day after tomorrow we are going to witness an amazing aurora borealis." At some of the blank stares, she added, "Northern lights. They should start in our area right after sunset and may go all the way into the wee hours of the morning. Grab your cameras and join me on the front lawn."

"Are we going to have a bonfire and roast marshmallows and make s'mores?" asked a young woman with a long brunette braid running down her back.

"No! No light," Jane insisted. "I'll even see if I can

have the lights around camp turned off early. That's why the Apostle Islands are perfect. We have no light pollution to interfere with nature's light show."

The same girl asked, "Well, when's our next fire?"

Ali answered the question. "Whenever you build a fire and bring the s'mores fixings, Sam. Check with Ed. He might have what you need for food."

Heath was glad Ali had said the girl's name.

"Okay, then, we'll have a fire tomorrow night," Sam declared. "The next night we'll watch the northern lights in the dark. As usual, it's BYOB. This means I'm making a run to Bayfield tomorrow. Get me your shopping list by breakfast."

After supper, as Heath and Ali walked back to their new cabin, he looked around for anywhere someone could hide. That was practically everywhere. Although the park service had lights on the corners of each building illuminating the paths between them, beyond those basic security lights was woods for at least a mile in each direction. There really wasn't anything he could do about that except perhaps install motion cameras. He'd add them to the list of things Kenner needed to do tomorrow.

"Do you need anything from the store for the fire tomorrow night?" Heath asked Ali. "Kenner will be coming out and installing cameras. I can ask him to bring anything you need. A bottle of wine? You seemed to like the vodka we had back at Bayfield base. Would you like him to bring some of that?"

"Thanks, I appreciate the offer, but I have my own little stash." Ali rested her hand on his bicep. As it was every time she touched him, his body flared with heat. He caught the end of her conversation. "It's with the other things that I'll move over into our cabin tomorrow morning before we leave for my testing rounds."

They reached the door, and Ali stood aside waiting for him to unlock it.

"Stay here." He entered first and quickly cleared the cabin, turning on several small nightlights. He remembered how she didn't like bright lights while she slept but appreciated the lantern in the bathroom tent. When she entered, he flipped on the overhead lights.

"What do you normally do in the evenings?" Heath asked.

"Usually, I have work to do in the lab. If you don't mind, I'm just going to change my shoes and grab a sweater." Ali looked at him with regretful eyes. "I'm really sorry, but I'm going to need to work for several hours this evening. Between my captivity and staying at the B&B, I'm nearly a week behind."

"No problem." And it wasn't for Heath. "Where you go, I go. It will give me an opportunity to look around the lab facility more."

He wandered the lab for the next five hours as Ali tested samples, worked on her computer, and occasionally spoke with other students. After each encounter, he quietly asked her about the student. He used his phone to make notes and immediately shared them with the Holt Agency, both locations. Finally, around midnight, Ali was yawning so hard her jaw made cracking noises. All the other students had left their stations, some telling her good night as they left.

"Ali, how much longer are you going to work?" He hated to see her work long hours like that.

She sat up and stretched, curving her back in a way

that thrust her breasts toward him. He wondered if she had any idea what that did to his body.

She glanced at her watch. "I was hoping to get more caught up." She stifled a yawn. "But I've got a full day tomorrow on the water, so I guess we'd better go to bed."

Heath looked around, confirming they were the last ones in the lab. "What do we have to do to shut down?"

"Nothing. The lab lights stay on all night. We have a couple of students who work at night." She gave him a small smile. "At least I think they're still here. One or two students were working on nocturnal animals before I got kidnapped."

Heath worried about how casually she spoke of her kidnapping. On his next land rotation, he would ask the psychologist the Holt Agency often used for women who were human trafficked or kidnapped. He'd see what she thought but might suggest to Ali that she speak with the psychologist via video call on her next day off.

Ali worked exceptionally efficiently, Heath noticed. She had very little to clean up or put away when she was finished.

He preceded her through every door, his hands on his weapon. At the cabin, he swept it once again, then declared it clear.

Once locked inside the building, Heath suggested, "Ali, why don't you go ahead and get ready for bed. When you're finished and under the covers, I'll get ready myself."

She gave him a tired smile. "Sounds like a good idea. I'll be asleep as soon as my head hits the pillow."

As Heath lay on his cot listening to each breath she took, he had a mental argument with himself. There was nothing in the Holt Agency personnel manual about becoming personally involved with a client. Several other agents had fallen in love while on a mission. The "don't fuck the job" rule was in the SEALs. He'd left the Navy almost four years ago. There was nothing keeping him from testing their chemistry. Except Ali. He'd have to be sure.

CHAPTER 16

THE NEXT NIGHT AFTER SUPPER, ALI FELT LIKE EVERYONE had made the same decision she did; to do their lab work until dark. There was a lot of chatter about the fire, especially from the newer students, some of whom had never been camping or experienced a campfire.

She spoke quietly to Heath so as not to embarrass herself or the other students. "I'm either getting very old or kids today aren't being exposed to the out-of-doors the way I was raised."

Heath smiled. "I was thinking the exact same thing. I can't believe how many of these kids are afraid of the fire. Don't they realize that's what that big, huge steel ring in the middle of the lawn is for? When we were kids, Robbie and I had to gather the big stones and place them in a circle, then hunt up the dry firewood and build a fire."

"Sam is quite comfortable in the outdoors. She's built several fires since she arrived. Unfortunately, she'll be leaving soon."

"Hey everybody, it's dark enough outside I'm going to

go ahead and light the fire." Sam looked around the lab. "Everybody's invited." She looked right at Heath and gave him a big smile. "You, too, Heath. If Ali doesn't have room on her blanket, you can cuddle on mine."

Jealousy streaked through Ali and landed in her heart. Sam was a beautiful woman, almost a decade younger than she was. Very athletic and extremely physically fit. She'd once told Ali that she normally ran at least three mudders every summer then explained that they were five miles of running, climbing and jumping over walls, sloshing through the mud and pools of water made in the woods. Ali considered herself very comfortable and adept in the wild but had no desire whatsoever to participate in anything like that.

Ali looked at her bodyguard whose light blue eyes were still on Sam. She couldn't read the look on his face. She was probably his version of the perfect woman. Just as she was about to tell Heath that he could go ahead and share Sam's blanket, he spoke.

"I'm sorry, Sam. I'm on duty." He turned warm blue eyes on Ali. Quietly so only she could hear, he said, "Far too young. I prefer my women to be closer to my age." His heated smile almost knocked her off her feet. "Do you have a blanket big enough for both of us?"

"Definitely. Let's go get it. You can pick the alcohol for tonight," she offered.

His smile never left his face. "No. You pick. I'm on duty."

"In that case, I'll have a drink for you." She wondered if there would ever be a time that they could have a drink together. Maybe while she was on her day off in Bayfield.

An hour later, sitting on her red plaid blanket, legs

stretched out in front of her next to Heath's long muscular legs, she poured them both a second drink. They were drinking cranberry and lemon lime soda. Only hers contained vodka.

"So, what do you think?" she asked as she handed him his red plastic cup.

"Brings back great memories. How about you?"

"I love campfires. We used to have small ones with my grandfather at the lake." She smiled at the memory. "Here, we'll often do them if someone who has been here several weeks is leaving. It's a nice sendoff."

Emma came bouncing toward them. "Heath, I'm making s'mores. Would you like one? I'm an expert at making them." She glanced at Ali and added, "How about you, Ali? I know how much you love s'mores."

"No, thank you," Heath replied.

"He prefers butterscotch and caramel," Ali told the young student. "But as you said, I love s'mores."

The heavyset girl with light acne smiled at her. "Lightly browned marshmallow. I know your order. I'll be right back." She'd only taken one step away when she turned toward Heath. "Next time we'll get some butterscotch and caramel."

He smiled back at the young woman. "You don't have to do that but thank you for thinking of it."

As soon as Emma was out of earshot, Ali noted, "You're quite the popular man tonight."

"While you were working in the lab, some of the students struck up conversations with me. They all seem very nice, at least the ones I've talked with." Although he thought he'd met everyone by that point, he hadn't spoken at length with several. That was on his to-do list. He'd sent his impressions back to both locations of Holt Agency as soon as the conversations were over.

Emma showed up with Ali's perfect s'more a few minutes later. After handing it to her as though it were a prize, the young college student bounced off.

"Have a bite." Ali offered in a sexy voice, and broke off a piece, handing it to Heath as warm marshmallow oozed down her fingers.

Even in the firelight she could see the heat in his eyes. "I'd love to." He leaned in and opened his mouth for her to feed him. More than willing to take advantage of the situation, Ali placed it in his mouth. He closed his lips around the morsel and her fingers. His tongue licked the warm sugar from her fingertips. "Delicious. Do you taste just as sweet everywhere?"

Her panties went instantly wet. Did he mean what she thought he meant? The double entendres had been flying between the two of them for days.

"Let me know when you're ready to go to bed." His voice was husky.

That was a blatant invitation unless she was severely mistaken. Well, she'd see. She chased the s'more with the last of her drink and started gathering their things.

"I'm ready now if you are." She chanced a glance at his crotch. Oh, yes. He was ready.

Heath stood and picked up the blanket, throwing it over his arm, casually covering his zipper and impressive erection. He looked at all the students before giving Ali a hand up. She bent down and grabbed the few things she'd taken to the fire.

Casually, they walked back to their cabin. He again went in first and cleared the open floor plan before coming back to the door to get her. As soon as she stepped in, he locked the door behind them just as he had for the last two nights. Tonight, though, he took the items from her hands.

"I'll take care of those," she protested as he set them on the floor.

"I'm not going to wait any longer." He placed his hands on the wall on either side of her head. "I've tried to talk myself out of this at least a dozen times a day. I've failed."

He leaned forward until his lips touched hers. She expected him to be hard and demanding given how alpha he was. But this kiss was tender, gentle. She opened for him and his whole body pressed hers into the wall.

Yes. That was her answer to him. Anything he asked of her. She wanted him.

Winding her arms around his neck, she took the kiss deeper, thrusting her tongue into his mouth, dueling with his for dominance.

His hands slid down to cup her ass.

She lifted her leg as though to climb him, needing to get closer.

"Wrap your legs around my waist," he ordered.

She raised the other leg as he cupped her bottom and lifted her with ease. He carried her all the way to her bed and sat down on the edge with her wrapped around him.

"I didn't think you wanted me," she admitted between kisses.

"What man wouldn't want you?" He kissed her long and hard. "I've wanted you ever since I found you in that horrible—"

She placed her finger over his lips, silencing him. "Let's not talk about that place right now." Moving her hands to the back of his head, she pulled it to her, kissing him thoroughly.

He found his way under her long-sleeved sweater and the T-shirt she wore underneath. The warmth of his hands on her bare back made her push lightly against them. He quickly unfastened her bra before moving his hands to the front and cupping her breasts.

It had been so long since a man had touched her. Far too many first dates, none of which she was willing to allow to touch her breasts. No one had ever caressed her as gently and tenderly as Heath did.

He moved his hands to her sides and ran his fingers up her skin, lifting her clothes off over her head.

He stared at her naked breasts. "Beautiful." His eyes met hers. "You're so beautiful, Ali. Perfect."

No, she wasn't, and she knew it. She was a thirty-three-year-old woman who taught high school students all day. She went to Pilates twice a week after school when she wasn't too tired, which meant she didn't make it to the studio very often. Here, on the island, she was surrounded by beautiful young women. Many, like Sam, who were better suited for a man like him. They could keep up with him. She'd bet he had run a mudder or two in his life or would be willing to do so.

Heath wiped his index finger across her wrinkled brow. "We don't have to go any further if you're not comfortable. If you want to stop, I—"

Once again Ali pressed her index finger over Heath's lips.

"There is nothing more than you that I want right now. But I don't understand why you would want me when there's a whole camp filled with young nubile women. I'm the oldest person in this camp."

"No, you're not. I am." With two fingers under her chin, he lifted her face and gently kissed her lips. He withdrew a few inches but held her gaze. "I have no interest in those young girls. In the spectrum of life, they are barely children. For most of them, this is their first life experience. What they fail to see is that this camp is truly still within the academic bubble. When I was their age, I had already done two missions in Afghanistan. If they had any idea the things I've done in my life, they'd consider me a monster."

"You're not a monster," Ali protested. "You're a goddamn hero." She placed her palms on his cheeks. "Look at me and listen to my words. You were a Navy SEAL. The best of the best. Everything you did was under orders in defense of our country. You're right. Those twenty-two, twenty-three, twenty-four-year-olds out there around the fire have no concept of the world you've lived in. Without even knowing what you've done, I'm so damn proud of you."

Ali ran her fingers through his blonde hair that curled above his ears and at the nape of his neck then leaned in and kissed him. When she broke the kiss, she grinned. "I'm old enough to know exactly what I want, and that's you. Inside of me. As soon as possible."

His smile made her body tingle, especially where her legs were spread in his lap. "I'll be more than happy to move this along, but I want to make sure it's what you want."

"I'm sure." She gave him a quick kiss. "Now, I believe you were about to suck on my breasts before my brain veered down an ugly path." She gave him another quick kiss. "Can we pick it up from there?"

"Oh, yeah." Heath leaned forward and took one of her breasts in his mouth while kneading the other very gently.

She wanted to touch his body. She reached to the hem of his polo shirt and started pulling it up when her fingers stumbled over the gun at the small of his back.

"Here, let me help you with that." With one hand at the back of his neck, he tugged off his shirt then pulled her to him. "I love the feel of your breasts on my bare chest." With him holding her tight, he whispered in her ear, "If my gun bothers you, I can get up and take care of it." He leaned back slightly to meet her eyes. "But I'd much rather take care of you."

He stood, with her legs and arms still wrapped around him. Turning, he laid her down on the bed. He knelt at the end and removed her boots before he unfastened her pants, pulling them and her panties off at the same time. He still wore his pants and boots, and his gun, while she was now completely naked.

He started at the arch of her foot and kissed his way up her legs, widening them to fit his shoulders. When he reached the apex of her thighs, he ran his finger down her slit then opened her to him with his thumbs. When his warm tongue licked the length of her open sex, Ali thought she was going to ignite and lift off the bed right then. His skilled tongue circled her clit before he took it into his mouth and sucked. She was helpless to do anything but lie there and enjoy his pleasurable torture. When he brought her to orgasm the first time, she wanted to scream in satisfaction but could only gasp his name.

By the time she crawled back from the best orgasm of

her life, Heath was already naked, condom on, and sliding onto the bed beside her. He brushed away a damp hair from her forehead. "Ready for number two?"

She blinked until he came into focus. "I'm ready for it to be your turn."

He traced her lips with a finger then ran it over her chin and down her throat, between her breasts and over her slightly rounded tummy before dragging all his fingers through her neatly trimmed hair. He dropped his middle finger over her sensitized clit then slid it into her wet channel.

"You're wet for me." He kissed her but didn't roll onto her. Instead, he picked her up and slid underneath her in the narrow bed, placing her astride his hips. "You felt tight. Has it been a while?"

Could this man get any more perfect? He was concerned about her comfort once again.

"It's been more than a while," she confessed. "It's been a long time. I told you that I've had a lot of first dates. Most of those never made it out of the batter's box."

He ran his thumb over her cheek. "We don't have to do this. We can stop right here and get on our pajamas. If you want me to, I'll simply hold you." He stared at her for a long second. "I just want to be near you."

Ali lifted her hips and guided him to her entrance. "Either you're big or all the other men I've been with have been below average."

"I don't want to hear about other men, especially as I'm about to slide into you." With his thumb he circled her clit, and she was wet again. "Take as much as you want."

Ali slid down a few inches and had to catch her breath. She'd never had a man that big, but she was bound and determined to take all of Heath. It was just going to take her a few minutes. When she was ready, she lifted up a little then pushed down further, taking more of him. On the third try, success. She lifted her hips and started to move. He played with her breasts, rolling her nipples between his thumbs and forefingers. The tighter he got, the closer she came to the edge.

"Let yourself go, Ali." She rose and lowered one more time and he lightly pinched her nipples. She flew over the edge. She felt him surge up into her a few more times before he grabbed her and pulled her down on top of him.

She never felt him slide out of bed to take care of the condom...any of the three times that night.

CHAPTER 17

"TEAM BRAVO CHECKING IN." HEATH KNEW HE WAS LATE but didn't give a damn. They'd made love three times last night, then again this morning as they showered together. Ali was an insatiable lover, but he wasn't going to complain.

"Is everything all right?" Kenner asked.

"Yes. We just had a campfire last night and stayed up late." Like all good lies, it was based in truth.

"Okay. Are you getting ready to head out now?"

"Within the hour. I believe we're heading to the central islands today. We'll give you confirmation when I call at the nine o'clock check-in." Heath looked at his watch. Fuck. It was already after nine. "I meant the noon check-in." He needed to change the subject away from him and Ali. "Anything new on the kidnappers?"

His friend grunted as though in pain. "No. Analysis came back last night on the chains and the handcuffs. Only Ali's prints. They could have been purchased anywhere. It's an extremely common chain sold in big box stores across the country. Farmers use it a lot on their gates because it's so thick and heavy. Construction sites are another frequent location. The FBI ran the voice through everything they had and came up empty."

"What about the drug?" Heath wanted to be able to give Ali some kind of good news.

"Xena is working on that. None of the pharmacies or physicians in a hundred-mile area are missing anything that could be hidden in food or water and put a hundred-and thirty-five-pound woman asleep for sixteen hours. A few of the pharmacists suggested some street drugs and Ryker has passed that on to his contacts in the DEA. I'm sorry that I don't have better news for you."

"I'm sure everyone on the team is doing everything they can. Thank you."

Ali walked into their bedroom area of the cabin. This morning they moved the two beds together. Since only the two of them had keys to the building, they decided to make themselves comfortable now that they were lovers. They would move his bed back when Xena came.

"Hey, Viper, Ali is ready to get started. We'll check in at noon. Bravo out." He took Ali into his arms. "Where to?"

"I think we'll do the Twin Islands today starting with North Twin. It's on the outer rim and one of the smaller islands." He kissed her before they left their personal sanctuary, locking the padlock on the outside of the door.

They went to the lab and picked up her equipment, stopped at the kitchen to grab their lunches, and went to the boat. They finished the first of the Twin Islands by lunchtime. Heath was about to suggest boat sex when they heard a boat engine.

He became instantly suspicious and grabbed the binoculars. "Who do you think that is?"

He handed the binoculars to her. "That's just Howard and Cliff. They're the ones doing bear research. Nice guys."

Heath was a little concerned when the boat came toward them. "It's definitely a research boat. Why would they be coming here?"

She cocked her head as if to say what the fuck. "To say hi. We're always friendly to one another, especially out here. Often, I'm by myself. It's nice to see a friendly face."

Although the Apostle Islands covered nearly seventy thousand acres, and they were only half a dozen research boats, Heath suddenly realized they'd never run into another research boat, or many other boats.

"Hi, Ali," Cliff yelled and waved as they approached. He tossed a line to her as they drifted together, motors idling.

"Hi, Cliff. Hi, Howard," Ali greeted the two men with a smile while Heath only watched. "I didn't think any bears were on North Twin."

"They aren't," Howard confirmed. "The U.S. Fish and Wildlife Services has a few game cameras on the island and asked us to swap out the SD cards. We were checking on a cub on Cat Island, so we came to handle this before we moved on to Rocky Island."

"Doesn't one of your dads work for fish and wildlife?" Ali asked.

"No. My dad's a hunting and fishing guide in Arizona." Cliff looked at Howard. "Doesn't your adopted dad work for forestry or something?"

"No. He drives a truck." Howard glanced at Heath

before he took the boat out of idle. "We still have a lot to do today and finding these game cameras isn't going to be easy." Howard flashed a smile. "Take care, Ali."

She threw the rope to Cliff. "Bye, Ali. Stay safe," he said.

Heath held Ali's gaze. "I'll bet they know these islands better than anybody else." It was a statement. Not a question.

"Yeah, probably. They have game cameras all over each of the islands."

"Fuck." Heath immediately pulled out his satellite phone and called Bayfield base.

"Bayfield base. Ryker here."

"Bravo team with new information. Hey, Ryker. Send Kenner and Xena back to the kidnap hut. Check for game cameras everywhere around it and on the way back to the lake. Take something to download an SD drive. We don't want them to know we've been there or know about their cameras."

"Fucking best lead we've had this whole mission. I'll send Kenner as soon as we're done talking. I'm sorry, Pitbull, but Xena won't be able to take over bodyguard duty. Her mother had to come to the United States. She's speaking to the United Nations in New York City then headed to the State Department for a week or so. Xena hasn't seen her in nearly a year and going to meet her in D.C. She's already left. If you need a break, I can send Kenner."

Ali had heard every word and was watching him with interest. "No need. I'm good. We may come back in a few days. Ali and I need to do laundry."

A huge smile broke over her face. Delight sparkled in her eyes.

"We just finished North Twin Island. Heading to South Twin. We may stop and drift while we have our lunch."

Suddenly he remembered the nervous glance Howard had given him. "One more thing, Ryker. See if somebody can dive a little deeper into Howard…" He couldn't remember the guy's last name or if Howard was his last name. He put his hand over the microphone. "Ali, what's Howard's full name?"

She shrugged. "I have no idea. To be honest, I don't know the full name of any of the students. Most of us just go by our first name or whatever the hell we want people to call us."

He quietly gave her a quick kiss before returning to his call. "I'm sorry, Ryker. Even Ali doesn't know his real name or full name, but he should be on the roster. See if he's related to somebody in fish and wildlife. He's adopted so you may want to check bio parents. It may not have come up in the original search."

"Hot damn. Another possible lead. Got anymore for me?"

Heath chuckled. "Not right now. Bravo out."

As soon as he ended the call, Ali jumped into his arms, wrapping her legs and arms around him, the same way she'd done last night. "You're not leaving me tomorrow." She kissed him hard and fast.

He immediately hardened. "Ever make love in a boat?"

That night at supper, a man in his mid-thirties sat down across from them.

He extended his hand. "Hi, I'm Anthony Morel. The new guy. Not really. I've been coming out here every year for at least a decade."

She slid her smaller hand into his and shook as she said, "Ali Frantz. And this is my bodyguard, Heath."

The man stared at him for a long moment before returning his gaze to Ali. Then he smiled. "Now I get it. Your father is Senator Jonah Frantz. Our senator and maybe the next president. I'm from Houghton."

Ali lit up. "I grew up in Marquette, at least for a little while."

Their conversation about the Upper Peninsula of Michigan and that part of Lake Superior continued throughout supper. Heath quickly noticed Anthony didn't wear a wedding ring nor did his ring finger look even slightly indented as though he'd recently taken one off. He caught bits and pieces of their conversation as he covertly texted Holt Agency base. He wanted to find out everything about this new man as fast as he could.

When he keyed back into their conversation, they'd moved on to high school students.

"I taught high school physics for a few years right after college but now I teach at Michigan Tech." The slightly graying thin man puffed out his small chest. "Most of my time is spent at the Great Lakes Research Center."

"Oh, do you know Professor…" Their conversation veered down the path of Ali's professors and her work.

Heath decided to ask a few questions of his own. "So, Anthony, or do you prefer Tony? Or something else?"

The man across the table from him smiled indulgently. "Anthony, please. I've never cared for that nickname."

"Very well then, Anthony, what's your research

project?" Heath was hoping it was something ridiculous and useless like hunting for the Lake Superior version of the Loch Ness monster.

Anthony moved his gaze away from Ali for the first time since he sat down. When their eyes met, he could read the man's body language. *Nothing but her stupid muscle. She's single and I'm going after her.* "I'm finishing my PhD in hydrology, specifically the study of erosion of the Apostle Islands caves."

"Interesting." That was all he said, biting his tongue about the oceanography classes he had to take as a SEAL, and reminding the short man that Lake Superior often acted like the ocean, right down to the fact the big lake had a tide.

He sat back and watched Ali and Anthony discuss multiple subjects with ease. The newcomer would be a perfect choice for a husband. He could see Meredith Frantz quickly accepting him as a future son-in-law. A well-educated professor from their home state of Michigan.

Heath was nothing more than a barely high school educated man who was medically retired from the SEALs. He'd been all over the world, in the worst places possible, but never traveled as a tourist.

Why the hell was he even thinking about Ali's future husband? It would never be him. He needed to back off. Give Anthony plenty of room to move in and sweep Ali off her feet.

Starting tonight at their aurora borealis watching.

After supper, Ali went to the lab to work for a few hours before sunset. It was no surprise to Heath that Anthony parked his ass in the closest available station to her. He seemed to have questions for her at least every ten to fifteen minutes. By the fifth time he interrupted her, Heath could tell her smile was not genuine. Was Prince Charming beginning to tarnish?

Jane flew into the lab, barely containing her excitement. "The sun is down, and Lady Aurora is already dancing. Grab your cameras."

Ali quickly picked up her area. "Let's go grab our blanket." She smiled up at Heath and slid a glance to Anthony who was still shutting down his computer. "See you out there."

She quickly walked to their cabin and slid inside before he even had a chance to clear it.

"Wait here and I'll go grab the blanket." He started toward the closet where it was stored. "You seem really anxious to see the northern lights."

"I've seen them before," she said from right behind him. "Living in the U.P., then spending summers up there, we saw them quite often." She didn't seem in any hurry at all.

"What's up? I thought you were all fired up to go see the lights."

She stepped in close to him and circled his neck with her arms. "I was all fired up to get away from Anthony... and to be alone with you." She went on tiptoes and kissed him.

He hesitated. Anthony would make her a good husband. They had so much in common.

"What's the matter?" she leaned back and asked.

"Are you sure it's me you want?" He most certainly wanted her and not just for sex. Ali had the toughest fortitude of any woman he'd ever met...other than Xena but she was one-of-a-kind.

He needed to give her the opportunity to possibly hook up with Anthony. "If you'd rather be with Anthony, I'll move my cot back to the other side of the wall. I can give you some privacy."

"Anthony?" She dropped her arms and took a step away. "Really?"

"The two of you seemed to get along so well." He tried to explain from his point of view. "You two talked nonstop during supper. It reminded me that I'm merely your body-guard. As such, I have to give you room to lead your life." He didn't like the distance between them, so he stepped closer to her.

He needed to touch her. Without hesitation he reached out and ran his thumb over her cheek. He didn't know what was happening between the two of them because they'd never discussed it. Or any future. "You are the most amazing woman I know. I don't know what this thing is between the two of us, and it's so new. Fragile." He pulled his hand away and let it drop to his side. "But if you wanted to get to know Anthony better, spend more time with him as a man, I'll give you that space." Under his breath he added, "It'll fucking kill me, but I'll do it."

CHAPTER 18

ALI STARED AT HEATH. SHE COULDN'T BELIEVE WHAT HE was suggesting.

"First of all, I have no interest in Anthony what's his name." She took a small step forward. "Yes, it was nice to talk to someone who grew up in the Upper Peninsula. Some of my fondest memories were of those years when Dad was just a state representative. Mother hadn't fallen off the deep end of society, Grandpa was still alive and the strong part of my life."

She took another baby step forward. "I have a high school student story to match every one of his and would have been happy to tell him, but he was more interested in my father." She shook her head. "Fending off questions about Dad is exhausting and frustrating. That's why I kept asking him questions. I was changing the subject. Supper felt more like another one of my first dates and you know I hate those fucking things."

This time she didn't stop. She stepped right into him and wrapped her arms around his waist. Thank God he enveloped her in his embrace. "Anthony drove me fucking nuts in the lab. That's my space to work which requires concentration. With him bothering me every fifteen minutes like a student hungry for attention, I didn't get hardly anything completed. Part of me is considering sneaking back into the lab to finish my work."

She smiled up at him. "Part of me wants to throw you on that bed and show you how much you mean to me. I don't know what this thing is between us either, but I want to give it time. I want to give *us* time."

When he lowered his head to kiss her, he whispered in her ear, "Christ, you're perfect." He kissed his way down her neck. His warm fingers had just curled under the hem of her sweater when they heard cheers and loud noises from outside.

Ali really wanted to go out there and see the beautiful spectacle as nature painted the night sky. "Let's go watch the northern lights."

"Okay. I haven't seen them in years." Heath led the way to the door. As he unlocked it, she remembered the blanket and trotted back to get it.

As he locked it behind him once they stepped outside, she made a decision. "Is there any reason we need to hide our relationship from these people?"

He thought about it for second. "None that I know of. I planned to tell my team when we spend the night in Bayfield."

"Good. We'll let them all draw their own conclusions, especially Anthony." Ali grabbed Heath's hand, walked to the middle of the yard, and spread out the blanket near several others. He sat down, knees and feet spread apart, and patted the space between his legs. She sat down in front of him and leaned her back against his chest. He immediately wrapped his arms around her middle.

"That should send the right message," he whispered in her ear.

When she giggled, several students in the vicinity looked their way. It would be all over camp by morning.

"Another one is starting," yelled Jane as she pointed.

Ali dug into the side pocket of her cargo pants and pulled out her phone. Instead of taking a picture of the aurora borealis, she took a selfie of the two of them. She'd remember the spectacular sight, but she wanted to keep the memory of tonight forever.

After watching nature's show for about an hour, the heat and hard proof of Heath's desire at her back, Ali'd had enough. What she wanted was poking her backside. "I've had enough. I must have two dozen pictures." She scooted forward and rolled to her knees then stood. Heath stayed on his heels as he gathered the blanket, standing with it once again in front of him.

He held out his left hand and she automatically took it, moving to that side.

Once again secured in their private cabin, they made love before snuggling to sleep.

She woke with the most delicious sensations. They were both on their left side, spooning, Heath behind her. His right hand was circling her clit. She was on the edge within minutes, her butt rocking back into his morning hard-on.

"Lift your leg."

She did as instructed and he slid a finger into her, testing her readiness.

"I love how wet you get for me." His words were as

much a growl as a whisper. "On any form of birth control? I'm clean. We're tested for everything every few months and I haven't been with anyone in nearly a year."

She giggled. "You already know it's been a long time for me. And to answer your question, yes, I have an IUD." She wished she was facing the other direction so she could see his face.

He probed her entrance with his cock. "Are you sure you're all right with this?"

There he went again. Always so concerned about her. "Positive. And if you slide in right now, you'll be able to ride my orgasm." As soon as he entered her completely, he lightly pinched her clit. That was all it took. She flew over the edge. He was right behind her as he drove in one more time.

"Perfect."

Ali was prepared for rude comments, general kidding, and questions as they stepped into the dining hall for breakfast the next morning. Howard and Cliff were the only two other people in the large dining facility.

"Good morning, Ed," she called cheerily to the cook. "Where is everybody?"

"Most of them stayed out until two o'clock in the morning taking pictures of the lights…and drinking. I don't expect to see many people until closer to noon. Making eggs to order this morning. How would you like yours?"

Howard and Cliff had already left by the time she and Heath sat down with their omelets, which were a real treat. There were usually too many students to individually cook breakfast.

Their days were filled with samples and sun, and their

nights were filled with passion. To Ali's surprise, no one ever said a word about their relationship, which grew stronger every day.

It was easier to think of Heath as her boyfriend rather than bodyguard. After several weeks, she wasn't sure she needed a bodyguard. But she needed Heath. She hadn't been threatened, but no one threatened her before she was kidnapped last time. She certainly wasn't going to complain about having him with her day and night. And oh, those nights. Thankfully the temperature dropped at night because their private little cabin didn't have any air-conditioning. He'd refused to open the windows to allow the natural breeze to cool their building, claiming it was too much of a security risk. The day Kenner brought over half a dozen fans, he became her favorite Holt agent...until Heath got hold of her that night.

Near the end of July, Jane announced at supper, "Since so many of us are leaving this weekend, I thought we would have big campfire Friday night. I'll make my last ever Bayfield run on Thursday so get your shopping lists as soon as possible."

"Do we need anything?" Heath asked. She loved the way that he had started referring to them as *we*. As though they were a real couple.

"No. We're good. Kenner brought several supplies when he came over earlier this week."

"How many more weeks before you're finished?" he asked when they were securely in their cabin.

She gave him her sassy smile. "Why? Ready to get rid of me?" She hoped not. She intended to ask her father to continue with Heath as her bodyguard back in D.C.

He pulled her into his arms and squeezed her tight. "I

don't want you to ever leave me." He buried his face in the crook of her neck. "Ali, what's going to happen to us at the end of summer?"

He picked her up as though she were a child and carried her to the bed, sitting down on the edge with her in his lap. "We've been living in a bubble where it's just been us. The only outside influences were young adults who really didn't give a shit what we were doing. We had our own cabin, our own boat, and a full-time cook. In just two weeks, we're going to have to return to real life." He gave her a soft kiss. "What do you see in your future?"

This was her chance to bounce the idea on someone else. "With my new master's, I'm thinking about looking for a job in a lab. Now, don't get me wrong, I enjoy my students and I love teaching. But teaching has changed so much since I graduated with my undergrad degree. The stuff they want us to do. The stuff we can't do anymore. The rules have become ridiculous. I just want to introduce science to young minds. Show them in the lab what can be done with the basic elements of our planet."

She turned to look into his light blue eyes, the ones she'd memorized over the past several weeks. "I feel like I can make a difference in a lab, doing research. Do you think I'm a fool to quit teaching?"

"I think you should do whatever your heart tells you to do. I can tell you from experience, being in a job you hate is miserable. There's no reason to be miserable when you have options."

Her mind repeated what he said, "follow your heart." "If I were to truly follow my heart, I'd ask you to run away with me to someplace nobody knows either of us. I'd continue my research on water. I find it fascinating. Freshwater holds the key to the future of the United States. All of mankind."

"Yeah. That's one of the things they pounded into our heads in SEAL training. The human body can't live long without freshwater."

"Exactly." It warmed her heart that he understood her passion for this research. Too bad her parents didn't. Mostly, her mother. Her father would want her to be happy and do whatever made her happy.

She gazed into the most beautiful blue eyes she'd ever seen. Heath made her happy. He made her laugh. He made her feel safe. He made her feel loved. Somewhere over the past several weeks together, she'd fallen in love with this big, kind, considerate man. She needed to find the right time to tell him that she loved him. He would never have made her mother's datable list, but he was at the top of her list.

She might have to ask Heath to marry her. First, though, she needed to tell him that she loved him.

"Hey, Ali, where did you go?" With his fingertips at the side of her temple, he gently pushed the hair away from her face and curled it around her ear. "I hope you made some decisions while you were there."

She leaned over and kissed him. "I most certainly did make some decisions."

"Do you want to share?" He raised his blonde eyebrows, bleached almost white in the summer sun.

"Not right now." She leaned in and kissed him again. She wasn't sure whether she deepened the kiss, or he did. It didn't matter. They ended up in bed, satisfying each other before they snuggled and fell asleep.

By the time Friday night rolled around, everyone in camp was so excited about the campfire.

Emma approached Heath on Thursday night, all smiles. "I was able to figure out a butterscotch and caramel s'more. I hope you like it. I'll be making it for you tomorrow night. Consider it my final gift to you."

"Emma, are you leaving?"

"Yes," she croaked out. "This has been the best summer of my life."

He smiled at the young woman who had changed a great deal. The sun and the wind had cleared up her skin. She may have lost a little weight but more important, she gained an amazing amount of confidence.

When she walked away, Ali had to say something to him. "You do know when you first got here, she had quite a crush on you."

He grinned at her. "Yeah. I know."

"Just you talking to her, treating her as the person she is inside, not the one people see when they first meet her. Thank you, Heath."

"She's really a good kid. Someday, some man is going to see that and treat her like the wonderful woman she is." He grinned. "Unfortunately for her, that man is not going to be me." He scooped Ali up and headed for the lab. "I have my hands full with you. And you have several hours of lab work to do tonight if we want the party tomorrow night at the campfire."

"I was wrong. You're not a wonderful man. You're a slave driver."

The next night as everyone gathered around the campfire, Danny played his guitar. It was surprising how many beautiful voices there were in the group. Liquor was passed and either splashed into a red plastic cup or passed on. Ali and Heath drank their vodka and cranberry with lemon lime soda, Heath's of course without the vodka.

Somebody handed Ali a s'more and Heath an original butterscotch caramel s'more.

That was the last thing she remembered.

CHAPTER 19

SENATOR JONAH FRANTZ RUSHED INTO HIS OFFICE LIKE usual. "Susan, my office, please." He picked up the pink slips from Shannon's desk. "Are any of these urgent?"

"No, sir. Just the usual."

He flipped through the pink slips with names and numbers. Nothing looked urgent.

"Susan, what do you have for me?"

"Sir, you need to leave in about five minutes for a vote on the green energy bill. I don't believe anybody will be surprised that you're voting against it. The party will be pleased because this is a tight one. But I'm not telling you anything you don't already know."

His phone buzzed with a text. He checked the caller ID and smiled. It was Annali. He swiped to see the picture she'd sent him today. He looked forward to the pictures she sent him every few days. Sometimes it was a sunset, other times it was something unusual she picked up in whatever samples. He never knew what to expect.

He opened the picture and stared at it for a few

minutes. It was a canoe in one of the Apostle Islands caves. Maybe she'd gone canoeing with some of her friends. She often talked about a new man in her life. He didn't care as long as she was happy.

The camera moved so he could see into the canoe.

"Oh, fuck. Not again." Jonah's heart squeezed. It must be somebody else. She had a bodyguard with her all the time.

"Sir, are you all right?" Susan was in front of his desk.

"Have Shannon get the Holt Agency on the line immediately," he yelled. "Where the fuck was Annali's bodyguard?"

Susan quickly instructed Shannon to make the call then she watched the video. "Sir, they probably killed her bodyguard to get to her."

"Jesus Christ, I hope not." He didn't want anyone's murder on his conscience.

He waited for the call he knew was coming. This time, he knew what to do, which buttons to push to record the entire conversation.

He was glad when the phone finally buzzed. He double checked to make sure that it was his Annali's phone. "What the fuck do you want this time?"

"Senator. Language. Last time you called me sweetheart when you answered the phone."

He didn't want to chitchat with this fucker who had kidnapped his daughter for the second time. "What is it you want me to do this time? I did what you asked last time. It wasn't my fault it didn't make it out of committee and onto the floor of the Senate. I'm still working on it, though." What the hell else could he want?

"Well, I thank you for that. I look forward to it making

it to the floor soon. But I have something much more urgent for you to do. You need to run to make it to the floor in time to vote yes on the green energy bill. Now, I know you were voting against it, but you need to vote *for* it. That is if you ever expect to see your daughter again. Right now, she's floating in a canoe in one of the many sea caves. She's been drugged with a very strong paralytic, which means she can see, hear, taste, but she can't move a muscle. Maybe her eyes, I'm not really sure. I have the antidote. You better hurry, Senator. You're going to have to run to make it there in time." The line went dead.

"Sir, I have Holt Agency online two," Shannon said from the intercom.

Jonah picked up the phone and jabbed the second line. "You let her get kidnapped, again. Susan is sending you the video and the phone conversation. Call me on my cell. I'm literally running to the Senate floor to vote on the bill the fucker wants me to vote yes on. It's against everything I believe in. Call my cell right now."

CHAPTER 20

HEATH WENT FROM A DEAD SLEEP TO WIDE AWAKE. KIND of. The first thing he did was reach across the cold bed for Ali.

She was gone.

Maybe he was still asleep and dreaming.

"Heath. Wake up."

That wasn't Ali's voice. It was a man's.

"Heath. We need you to wake up." What the hell was Ryker doing in their bedroom? "You need to fight the drug. Does he need another dose?"

"I've given him more than any man is supposed to get. This is an animal tranquilizer and I'm a human doctor. I think they gave him too much. Maybe it was supposed to kill him."

"Fuck."

Kenner was here, too? This was one hell of a bad dream. "Give him more. He's big and he's tough."

"Heath. Squeeze my hand again."

Ryker and his damn orders, but he was the boss.

Heath tried with all his might to squeeze as hard as he could the hand that was holding his.

"Good job. Keep fighting the drug. We need you to help us find Ali."

He ran his hand over the cold sheets next to him. She wasn't there. Maybe she was in the bathroom. He listened and heard only boots shuffling and occasional mumbling.

"Go ahead, Doctor. Give him more," Ryker ordered.

More of what? He felt warmth moving up his arm. Or was it cold? When it hit his head, he opened his eyes and blinked. It was as though his brain suddenly woke up. His whole body tingled as if he hadn't moved all night. Heath stretched.

"That's a very good sign. I think he's coming around."

Heath focused his eyes. "What the fuck are you two doing here?"

"Ali's been kidnapped, again," Ryker explained. "You were drugged with an animal paralytic. We need your help to find her."

Fear shot to his heart, pushing whatever the doctor gave him through his system faster. Heath fought to clear his brain.

Ali was gone.

Heath sat up on the edge of the bed and realized he had an IV in his arm.

"We're going to push a bag of ringers like we did in the Navy. Brace," Kenner warned just before he squeezed the clear bag. "Go pee. We need you to clear the shit out of your system as fast as we can."

"Sit rep," Heath managed to ask for a situational report as he trudged to the bathroom. His whole body felt like it was weighed down. His bladder was so full he almost went a little with every step.

"Senator Frantz got the call forty-five minutes ago. He was able to delay the Senate vote on the green energy bill until this afternoon. Everyone thinks it was postponed for some other reason, so the kidnapper won't know."

"Show me the picture and play the video. I can multi-task here."

After the longest piss he'd ever taken in his life, he'd heard the phone conversation twice while staring at the video of Ali. He didn't know he was crying until after he'd washed his hands. He went to splash water on his face and noticed in the mirror that it was already wet.

He swallowed down his emotions before returning to their bedroom to get dressed as quickly as he could. His brain was clearing more each minute. Cave. Where the hell would Anthony be? Might he be able to recognize it? He sure as hell hoped so.

As soon as he tied his boots, he stood. He swayed slightly and hoped nobody else noticed it, but Kenner grabbed his arm.

"I've got you, Pitbull."

"Let's check the lab for Anthony. He's been working for years on the caves here in the Apostle Islands. He knows more about them than any man on earth."

"Wait a fucking minute." Ryker stopped walking. "Could he be our kidnapper?"

"Keep walking," Heath insisted. "No. He wasn't here when she was kidnapped the first time. He showed us pictures of him leading a team of students through caves on the Yucatán Peninsula in Mexico. I checked the airlines to be sure."

He scanned the lab as soon as he entered. A few students were at the far end with their heads down and earbuds in. Typical. Anthony was at the table space he'd claimed. Excellent!

"Anthony, need your help," Heath said as he approached the man he once thought would be an excellent husband for Ali.

Ryker stepped up and kept his voice low so the students could hear. "Everything we're about to tell you is for your eyes and ears only. It's beyond top-secret. I'd have you sign a confidentiality statement but we're in too much of a rush."

The man looked like a deer in headlights. "Sure, anything I can do. What do you need from me?"

Heath was on the other side of Anthony and keyed up the video on his phone. "Ali has been kidnapped. We were both heavily drugged. What you're about to see isn't going to be easy to watch. I need you to carefully observe the background and tell me if you have any idea where she could be."

Anthony nodded. "Okay. I understand."

As soon as her body was visible, the university professor released an animalistic cry. "No!" His shoulders shook as tears flowed.

The students at the other end of the lab looked toward Anthony as the team from Holt Agency surrounded the professor.

"Pull it together, man." Kenner had Anthony by the shoulders and shook him. "We need your help. Do you recognize the cave?"

"I hate to do this but I need to see it again." Two seconds into the video, Anthony asked to pause it. "Can we plug your phone into my computer so I can enlarge this?"

"No, but I'll email it to you." His phone had too much classified information on it to be connected to anything other than a Holt computer.

It took nearly a minute for Heath's satellite phone to download the video. He hated even that short of time to be wasted. They had to find Ali.

Anthony stared at the still frame for what seemed like forever before announcing, "This is Devils Island."

"Are you sure?" he asked.

"Look, Anthony, I don't know you." Ryker moved in a few inches. "You're going to have to explain to me why you think this is Devils Island rather than any one of the hundred other caves."

"That's easy." With a pencil in his hand he pointed to layers of the cave. "See these layers? There's greater erosion than..." He grabbed an eight- by ten-inch color picture from a drawer on top of his desk. "Right here on Stockton Island." He grabbed another picture. "This was from a cave on Madeline Island." He opened another drawer and pulled out another photograph. "And this one's from Sand Island. As you can see this one seems similar because they're both outer ring islands, but if you look closely where Ali is being held captive, you'll see this unique lighter band. Because Devils Island takes a beating being the furthest out, its caves are eroded considerably more."

"That helps us some, but Devils Island has lots of caves." Heath was pleading with the man he once considered his rival. "Is there any way to pin down which side?"

"Certainly. It's on the west side. Western caves are

carved deeper than those on the east side because prevailing winds are from the west, thus storms come from the west." The professor pulled down a map.

Ryker spoke to Heath. "Is there any reason we need him?"

"I can help you pin the correct cave down quicker." Anthony stood up.

"Do you have everything you need, professor? We're leaving right now." Ryker turned and strode out of the building, never slowing until he stepped onto the boat he'd brought over from Bayfield. It was a large cabin cruiser but configured for speed, not research.

Heath offered his hand to the doctor but the man, a decade older than him, waved him off. "This is my boat. I might be the only doctor in Wisconsin who still makes house calls. You'd be amazed how often people get hurt in these islands. By the way, I'm Dr. Troy Ware." They shook hands briefly before the doctor stood behind the wheel and backed the boat away from the dock with the ease of familiarity.

"Hang on," the doctor warned as he gunned the engines and brought the boat up on plane in seconds. He maneuvered through the inner islands with expertise, arriving at Devils Island in what Heath considered record time.

"Anthony," Ryker called. "You're up."

"It's none of these," the professor said with confidence. "But it's not as far down as the lighthouse."

As they came around a large outcropping the size of a strip mall, they noticed a research boat sitting out in the water two thousand yards, just floating. It immediately fired its engines and headed directly for them.

Heath grabbed his binoculars. "The way he's coming at us, I don't think he wants to say hi."

"These are the caves," Anthony shouted. "I think she's in one of these."

"So do I," Heath agreed without taking his eyes off the research boat.

The doctor pulled in closer and slowed down to a crawl.

"Well, professor, can you tell the difference between any of them?" Ryker asked.

"I'm sorry, but there really isn't that much difference between them." He pointed to the motorized canoe strapped onto the stern. "If we take that canoe, I might be able to help."

"Thank you, professor," Ryker said as he and Kenner headed for the canoe. "You've been extremely helpful. You got us to where we needed to be."

Heath never lost sight of the research boat fast approaching. "Oh, shit. Gun!" he screamed at the top of his lungs. "Everybody down."

Heath ducked and opened his weapons duffel. In less than one minute he had his long rifle assembled. SEALs were trained in shooting from a small boat. Through the powerful scope on his sniper rifle, he put the man in the research boat in his crosshairs.

"Fuck. I never would have guessed it was him."

"Shoot to injure," Ryker ordered. "We need him alive."

Heath took the shot.

Cliff spun away from the wheel and disappeared into the bottom of the boat that was still traveling at maximum speed toward them.

Before Ryker could ask, Heath said, "Clean shot to the

left shoulder. He had the gun up to his right. He spun away from the wheel and must have fallen to the floor." They all knew that didn't mean that the tango was out of the game. Somalian pirates often used that trick and then shot at them, protected by the side of the boat. Without getting higher to be able to see down into the boat, they were blind.

"Doc, get us out of here," Ryker ordered.

The doctor moved their boat away a few hundred feet.

They all watched as the research boat crashed into one of the many pillars that defined the caves.

Dr. Ware immediately headed to the crash site.

"Kenner, you're with the doctor." Ryker headed toward the back of the boat and the powered canoe. "Heath, let's go get your woman."

It only took them a few minutes before they were motoring into the caves that lapped loudly with waves caused by the crash and their own boat. The canoe cut amazingly well through the turbulent water. They had to travel deep into each cave looking for Ali and the canoe. If the waves had knocked her out of the canoe, she wouldn't be able to save herself with the paralytic drug in her system.

They rounded the next wall.

"There she is!" Heath yelled and his voice echoed through the hollow caves. "You missed Ali's lecture, but this water is much deeper than you think."

Ryker's brows drew together. "It can't be any more than three feet."

Heath laughed. "Don't be a fool. It's easily fifteen feet. Bring our canoe next to hers. I'm not sure will be able to transfer her to this boat without all of us ending up in the water. I don't think you can counterbalance the two of us."

"Tie her to us. We can drag her boat back to the hospital boat. They have a lift at water level."

Heath wanted nothing more than to crawl into the boat with Ali and hold her, but it might have put both of them in danger.

Ten minutes later, they were all back on the doctor's boat. Ali and Cliff were both down in the cabin, which had been configured as an emergency room.

As Ryker and Kenner lifted the canoe back into place, he'd made it to the cabin in three long strides. "Dr. Ware, how is she?"

"I've administered the first shot of antidote and I'm getting ready to hook her up to ringers to help wash it out of her system." He glanced up and grinned. "Unlike you, we're not going to push it. Her body's been through enough. We're going to let it recover at its own speed."

As soon as he had Ali set up, he turned to Cliff lying on the other bed. "You call it. Left shoulder. Clean shot. A through and through but since it was such a huge caliber, tore the hell out of his shoulder. I've already called for him to be airlifted. Chopper should be here soon. I also called in the crash. Coast Guard is on its way. All five of us saw the same thing. He had a gun. You defended us."

"If he's awake, I need to ask him some questions," Ryker said from the door, Kenner right behind him with his phone ready to video everything.

"He's stabilized. I can wake him." The doctor injected something into Cliff's IV.

He woke up with a start. "You're not going to take her

again. I won't let you." His good arm flailed around as if he was looking for the gun.

"Why did you kidnap Annali Frantz?" Ryker had been one of the best interrogators on their entire SEAL team.

"I needed her father to do as I say. I knew if Senator Frantz thought I was going to hurt his only daughter, he'd do anything I asked."

"Is that why you kidnapped her the first time?" Ryker was really good.

"Yes. I need the national park rangers to make more money. See, two years ago, during the last budget cuts, my dad got his hours cut to part-time. That's why he has to be a hunting and fishing guide. Because of the recession, which is Congress's fault, even the guiding service has dropped off so much that he can't afford to pay for my college tuition anymore. I'm going to have to quit in the middle of my master's program."

"Why did you want the senator to vote yes on the green energy bill?" Ryker asked the young man on the bed.

"There's money in there for the national parks and to refund the grant for Howard and me."

"Well, Cliff, you're not going to have to worry about college or your research anymore." Ryker crossed his powerful arms over his broad chest. "You know what the penalty is for kidnapping the child of a member of Congress?"

The young man began to shake. "No."

"Life in prison or the death penalty. And you did it twice, making demands of a member of Congress. One who just might be our next president. You think about that as a policeman handcuffs your good arm to a bed the whole time you recover."

Heath had been holding Ali's hand since he entered the boat cabin. He felt her twitch. "Dr. Ware, I think she's coming around."

"Interview over," Ryker announced, and he turned toward Ali's bed.

"That's good," the doctor said as he stepped to her bed and checked the machines. "Try to wake her. She might need just a little bit more. This is a very powerful drug."

"Yeah, it is. It's what we use on bears so we can tag them or check their tags." Cliff glared at Heath. "I thought I gave you enough kill you. I didn't think anybody would try to find Ali for at least a day."

Ryker looked to Kenner. "Did you get that confession of attempted murder?"

Kenner smiled. "Oh, yeah. They hate to be ignored after the interview."

"But...but you said the interview was over. You can't use that against me?" Cliff protested.

"I can do anything I want. I don't carry a badge." Ryker smiled two rows of white teeth at the young man on the bed.

"Ali, time to wake up," Heath encouraged. "Please, Al, show me those beautiful brown eyes." He traced her face with his fingertips. "You have to wake up. I have something very important to tell you."

She didn't move for several minutes.

"As I thought. She's going to need a little more." The doctor injected something into her IV. "Give it ten more minutes to get to her and through her system."

Ryker perked up. "Choppers. Sounds like two." He swung his gaze to Dr. Ware. "Does Ali need to be medevacked?"

The doctor looked confused. "No. I only called for one helicopter."

Ryker, Kenner, and Dr. Ware went up on deck. A state policeman came back down with them and went directly to Cliff's bed. After going through the procedures, Cliff was read his rights. Two people from the helicopter crew came in and left with Cliff. A minute later, a man and a woman in suits came into the cabin.

The woman spoke first. "FBI." Both the newcomers flashed badges. "Dr. Ware, can we report to the senator and to the Senate chamber that his daughter has been rescued and is in good health?"

"As you can see, she's still unconscious. She's suffered minor exposure and is being treated. She just received her second injection of antidote to the bear paralytic she was admittedly given by the man who was just carried out of here."

Ryker spoke from behind them. "Yes, you can report to the chamber that Annali Frantz has been rescued and they can go ahead with the vote. I will personally be calling Senator Frantz when you leave."

She gave him a small smile. "I will personally report to Senator Frantz that I have seen his daughter and she is in good hands." She held out her hand to him. "Nice seeing you again, Ryker. Please tell Xena I said hi."

His returning smile was genuine. "Several of the women you two trained with are coming to the farm in two weeks. You should consider joining them, Erica."

"I'll call Xena and get the details," she said as she walked out the door. A few seconds later, Heath heard a helicopter buzz overhead then fly off.

"I thought Erica was a man when I watched the two of

them fast rope down from the helicopter," Kenner admitted.

"Wait until you meet the rest of Xena's friends." Ryker grinned.

Ali stirred.

"Doc, we have more movement," Heath said with a smile.

Dr. Ware nodded. "Looks like she's going to come out of it this time. Goddamn bear tranquilizer. He could have easily killed her with the wrong dosage."

Heath looked up at him. "Or killed me, with the right dosage."

"I don't think he was the brightest crayon in the box." Ryker shook his head. "I'm always amazed when bad guys don't think they're going to get caught."

"Heath, what time is it?" Ali asked just above a whisper as she rolled to her side facing him. Still holding his hand, she cuddled into it.

"Ali, I need you to wake up. You've been asleep for long time." He didn't want to tell her she'd been kidnapped again because that had been her greatest fear.

"Okay. I'm awake." She tried to sit up. "I think I might be sick. All I want to do is sleep. That's the way I get when I'm sick." She laid back down.

"She can stay there," the doctor said. "As soon as the Coast Guard gets here, we can head home. She'll probably recover quicker in her own bed."

A few minutes later, large boats were heard outside. Everyone but Heath left.

"Ali, I need to talk to you."

She took a deep breath and opened her eyes. "Are you sick, too?"

He grinned. "Not anymore, but I was this morning." He gathered her into his arms and pulled her onto his lap. "Ali, I've never been so scared as I was this morning. I thought I was going to lose you, and I just found you. I'm never gonna let you go. I love you too much."

She nuzzled into his neck. "Good, because I was going to ask you to marry me."

Heath lifted his head and looked down at the woman in his arms. Was she under some kind of truth serum?

In that half-asleep voice of hers, she continued. "I've known for some time that I love you. I don't care if my parents like you or want you to be my husband." She sat up and looked him in the eye. "I'm a thirty-three-year-old woman. I can make up my own mind about who I want to marry and where I want to work. Are you still okay if I want to go to work in a lab?"

"I'm okay with whatever you want to do as long as you're okay with my job."

She put her palms on his cheeks and leaned in and kissed him. "I'm so damn proud of what you do. Rescuing people...like me. Go rescue the world." She kissed him quickly. "Then come home to me."

Heath leaned forward and kissed her with all the love he felt in his heart.

"Can we get married before we tell my parents?"

EPILOGUE

"WELL, THAT WENT BETTER THAN I THOUGHT IT WOULD," Heath admitted as they left the Frantz home in Washington D.C. He'd been dreading that night since Ali had agreed to marry him.

"I think Dad was happy that we're moving to Michigan." Ali slid into the passenger seat of Heath's two-year-old decked-out pickup truck. His uncles would have called it a country Cadillac. His new wife smiled at him and his entire being warmed. Good thing it wasn't a long drive to their current home in the Virginia suburbs. He loved making love to his wife.

"Did you see my mother instantly accept you as soon as you said you were a former Navy SEAL? I bet you right now she's on the phone to all her friends bragging about her new son-in-law."

"Sucker bet. I think your father was pleased when we told him we'd eloped." He merged onto the Beltway and headed toward Virginia.

"Dad knew a wedding would turn into a huge political

event with everyone asking him if he intended to run for president."

"And cost him a fucking fortune," Heath added.

"I hope Mother listens to me for once and keeps this reception small. I can't thank you enough for agreeing to a Las Vegas wedding." Ali leaned over and kissed Heath's cheek.

"I'm a guy. I didn't give a shit where we got married." He glanced over to the love of his life riding shotgun. "As long as I ended up with you in my life forever, as soon as possible."

"That was such a pretty little chapel outside of the city. I couldn't handle an Elvis wedding." Ali visibly shivered. "I couldn't believe all your Holt Agency friends and their wives wanted to come."

"I was surprised as hell that Tavis and Colette, Grant and Callie, as well as Holden and Melanie all flew in from D.C." On second thought, yes, he could. All the men had been through hell and back together; first as a SEAL platoon, then as prisoners of war in Ethiopia. Those bonds held hard. "I'm excited about going to Tavis's house next week and seeing all the men who now live here in Washington. We didn't have much of a chance to talk at the wedding." He grinned at the windshield. He had other things on his mind that day than catching up on old times.

"Serena did a fantastic job making all the arrangements within days. She handled everything precisely to my wishes. I still feel terrible about dumping everything on her but I had to finish all my reports or I wouldn't have completed the courses."

Heath snickered. "That woman could arrange for an

entire Marine battalion to invade a country all while entertaining their baby."

"I wish Serena was planning the party to introduce us next weekend instead of my mother. At least she'd listen to what I wanted." Ali watched her princess-cut diamond ring and gold wedding band sparkle under the streetlights. "Have I told you how much I love my wedding set?"

He chuckled. "You should, you picked it out," he reminded her.

"But you helped. I love that you added the blue sapphires on each side of the diamond. Every time I look at my hand, I'll be reminded of the two months we spent on Lake Superior falling in love."

"We'll see plenty of Lake Superior over the next several years. As soon as we sell your condo, I think we need to look for a house on Lake Superior. Something close enough that you can easily drive to Houghton, even in the winter."

She slowly shook her head side to side. "I still can't believe Anthony helped me get into the PhD program at Michigan Tech, and that I get to work at the Great Lakes Research Center continuing the work from this summer."

"Ali, your rescue traumatized the hell out of him."

"I suppose." She grinned at him from across the truck. "When we go back to the Apostle Islands next summer, do you think we can have our private cabin again?"

"Why would I need to go?" Heath slid her a glance. "Are you planning on getting kidnapped again?"

"I'm sure Dad would understand if I told him I'd rather have you guarding me than Secret Service."

The end.

MORE BOOKS BY KALYN COOPER

Holt Agency

THE HOLT AGENCY IS A SPINOFF FROM BECCA JAMESON'S and KaLyn Cooper's Shadow SEALs books. The group of rescued SEALs have opened their own agency.

Rescued by Becca Jameson ~ Tavis is a former Navy SEAL. He's not a babysitter. But when the Secretary of State hires you to guard his daughter, no is not an acceptable answer. Starting a relationship with the woman he's supposed to protect would get him fired. It would also leave her vulnerable.

Unchained ~ Living on the farm in the middle of nowhere, working in a tiny town, was perfect for Kelly and her son. For the first time in their lives, they both felt safe. When Kelly's past catches up with her, can Keene save her and Jock...and his heart?

Protected by Becca Jameson ~ Someone is after her. She might not like it, but she needs Holden's protection. The two of them can try to keep their feelings for each other at bay, but for how long?

Liberated ~ She was the job and off limits, but his heart wanted so much more. You know what they say about best laid plans. Will they work out right this time for Heath and Ali?

Defended by Becca Jameson ~ There was no way he would leave Anya to her own defenses. He had the means and the space to help her. Now all he needed was a dose of self-control. Would it be so bad if he let her lean on him in her time of need?

Unrestrained ~ Crossover with Ladies of Black Swan, Team 2

Black Swan Series

Military active duty women secretly trained in Special Operations and the men who dare to capture the heart of a Woman Warrior.

Unconventional Beginnings Prequel (Black Swan novella #0.5) ~ He's dead. But they can't allow it to affect her. She's too important.

Unrelenting Love: Lady Hawk (Katlin) & Alex (Black Swan novel #1) ~ Women in special operations? Never… Until he sleeps with the most lethal woman in the world.

Noel's Puppy Power: Bailey & Tanner (A Sweet Christmas Black Swan novella #1.5) ~ He's better at communicating with animals than women, but as an amputee she knows firsthand it's the internal scars that can be most difficult to heal.

Uncaged Love: Harper & Rafe (Black Swan novel #2) ~ The jungle isn't the only thing that's hot while escaping from a Colombian cartel.

Unexpected Love: Lady Eagle (Grace) & Griffin (Black Swan novel #3) ~ He never believed in love, but he never expected to find her.

Challenging Love: Katlin & Alex (A Black Swan novella #3.5) ~ A new relationship can be fragile when outsiders are determined to challenge that love.

Unguarded Love: Lady Harrier (Nita) & Daniel (Black Swan novel #4) ~ She couldn't lose another sick baby… then he brought her his dying daughter.

Choosing Love: Grace & Griffin (A Black Swan novella #4.5) ~ Hard choices have to be made when parents interfere in a growing relationship.

Unbeatable Love: Lady Falcon (Tori) & Marcus (Black Swan novel #5) ~ Scarred outside and in, why would his beautiful friend ever want more with him?

Unmatched Love: Lady Kite (Lei Lu) & Henry (Black Swan novel #6) ~ Scarred outside and in, why would his beautiful friend ever want more with him?

Unending Love: Lady Falcon (Tori) & Marcus (Black Swan novel #7) ~ Their life together is not over. He has to believe it…or it will be.

Undefeated Love: Katlin and Alex (Black Swan novel #8) ~ Where all the questions are answered.

Guardian ELITE Series

Former special operators, these men work for Guardian Security (from the Black Swan Series) protecting families in their homes and executives on the road, but they can't always protect their hearts.

ELITE Redemption (Guardian ELITE Book 1) ~ Guarding a billionaire and his wife isn't easy when you can't keep your eyes off your bikini wearing, gun carrying partner who is lethal in stilettos. *This book was previously published as **Double Jeopardy**.*

ELITE Justice (Guardian ELITE Book 2) ~ She's not what she seems. Neither is he. But the terrorist threat is real. So is the desire that smolders between them. *This book was previously published as **Justice for Gwen.***

ELITE Rescue (Guardian ELITE Book 3) ~ When Jacin awoke stateside, he remembered nothing about his escape from the Colombian cartel or his torture. He was sure of only one thing, his love of Melina, his handler. When she disappears, neither bruises nor the CIA will keep him from rescuing her. *This book was previously published as Rescuing Melina.*

ELITE Protection (Guardian ELITE Book 4) ~ Terrorists want her…but so does he. The chase isn't the only thing that heats up when the flint of the former SEAL strikes against the steel of the woman warrior. *This book was previously published as Snow SEAL.*

ELITE Defense (Guardian ELITE Book 5) ~ Guarding her wasn't his job, but he couldn't let her die…even before she stole his heart. When he discovers the temptingly beautiful foreign service officer is being threatened, his protective instincts take over. *This book was previously published as Securing Willow.*

ELITE Damnit (Guardian ELITE Book 6) ~ With a hurricane bearing down on the tiny island, they only have days to find and rescue ten kidnapped young girls and their chaperones…and keep their hands off each other. *This book was previously published as a short story titled Damnit I Love You.*

Suspense Sisters

SEAL in a Storm ~ This sizzling military romance features a seasoned hero and heroine, second chances, and edge of your seat suspense. SEAL in a Storm is part of the Suspense Sisters new wave of connected books, Silver SEALs.

Shadow in the Mountain Another mission into the shadows was the last place he wanted to be. Last time it ended his career. This time promises death or salvation.

Shadow in the Daylight After he left the SEALs, Andrew did a covert job for Charley before parting ways. As the Security Officer aboard a cruise ship, he invited several

SEAL friends to travel as his guests through the Panama Canal. He never imagined he'd need their highly trained skills.

Cancun Series

Follow the Girard family —along with their friends, former SEALs and active duty female Navy pilots—as they hunt Mayan antiquities, terrorists and Mexican cartels in what most would call paradise. Tropical nights aren't the only thing HOT in Cancun.

Christmas in Cancun (Cancun Series Book #1) ~ Can the former SEAL keep his libido in check and his family safe when the quest for ancient Mayan idols turns murderous?

Conquered in Cancun (Cancun Series Book #2) ~ A helicopter pilot's second chance at love walks into a Cancun nightclub, but she's a jet fighter pilot with reinforced walls around her heart.

Captivated in Cancun (Cancun Series Book #2) ~ His job is tracking down terrorists so he's not interested in a family. She wants him short-term, then needs him when their worlds collide.

Claimed by a SEAL (Cancun Series crossover Book #4 with Cat Johnson's Hot SEALs) ~ How far will the Homeland Security agent go to assure mission success when forced undercover for a second time with an irresistible SEAL?

Never Forgotten Trilogy

The mission brought the five of them together, disaster nearly tore them apart, a mystery and killer reunited them forever.

A Love Never Forgotten (Never Forgotten novel #1) ~ Dreams or nightmares. Truth or lies. He can't tell them apart. Then he discovers the woman who has haunted his dreams is real. Is she his future? Or his past?

A Promise Never Forgotten (Never Forgotten novel #2) ~ As a Marine Lieutenant Colonel, he could take on any mission and succeed. Raising his two godchildren…with her…just might kill him.

A Moment Never Forgotten (Never Forgotten novel #3) ~ The moment he realized she was in serious danger…he couldn't protect her.

ABOUT THE AUTHOR

KaLyn Cooper is a USA Today Bestselling author whose romances blend fact and fiction with blazing heat and heart-pounding suspense. Life as a military wife has shown KaLyn the world, and thirty years in PR taught her that fact can be stranger than fiction. She leaves it up to the reader to separate truth from imagination. She, her husband, and Little Bear (Alaskan Malamute) live in Tennessee on a micro-plantation filled with gardens, cattle, and quail. When she's not writing, she's at the shooting range or paddling on the river.

For the latest on works in progress and future releases, check out **KaLyn Cooper's website**
http://www.kalyncooper.com/

Follow **KaLyn Cooper on Facebook** for promotions and giveaways
www.facebook.com/KaLynCooper1Author

Sign up for exclusive promotions and special offers only available in **KaLyn's newsletter**
kalyncooper.com/newsletter

Made in the USA
Thornton, CO
05/26/23 16:41:35

b7ac5bfe-6b01-4524-a4a9-925c3681ae52R01